Bed & Breakfast in Charlford

Bed & Breakfast
in
Charlford

W. Henry Barnes

Copyright © 2023 W. Henry Barnes

All rights reserved

Paperback **ISBN:** 9798392771028
Hardback **ISBN:** 9798392782369
Imprint: Independently published

Dedication

Everything I have ever done has been for all my family who always supported me in my plans, career paths and hobbies. For my venture into writing fiction, my thanks go mainly to my lovely wife Margaret who encouraged me and gave me the freedom and the time that the books demanded. But I doubt if the books would have gone beyond manuscripts if son Ian hadn't helped me with his knowledge of literature and experience of publishing over the Internet. Son David, with Susi's support, nursed me back to health after Margaret was snatched from us by a massive stroke. The growing musical career of granddaughter Laura (Lo Barnes) fills me with admiration and hope. My love goes to them all and to Margaret's family.

Chapter 1

The Plan went into operation that Friday in the middle of August. They could have aborted it at any time up to half past four that day, but they didn't – didn't even consider the possibility. But if they'd foreseen the impact it would have on their lives, and on the lives of others, then at least one of them might have chickened out.

It started as they left their home town of Bracknell on a series of buses and coaches that would take them towards the heart of the West Country and a village near the city of Salchester. Public transport provided both camouflage and anonymity – they would be seen simply as three teenagers in jeans and T-shirts with a variety of sports bags, backpacks, carrier bags and guitar cases. But, having visited the target area in the past, they felt they ran the risk of being recognised and accosted in the last stage of the journey. So, keeping to The Plan, they left the final bus a couple of miles short of their destination and completed the approach along footpaths through fields and woods.

This part of the journey was critical – the aim now was to remain unrecognised whilst trying not to act suspiciously. However, from earlier visits to the area, they believed there was little chance of bumping into walkers, and any farm workers would be too busy to pay much attention. All this had gone into the preparation of The Plan – Slim's attention to detail, while attracting some adverse comments during that preparation phase, was being vindicated.

Their final approach to the target village, Charlford, was along a path skirting a wood where they were hidden from view by the unkempt hawthorn hedge to their left. Nearing the end of the path, where the road came into sight, they paused, looked out, and listened. Nothing and nobody seemed to be moving in the soft dusty warmth of the summer afternoon.

Whacker, about to step into the road, was grabbed and held back. 'What's wrong, Slim? Come on, let's go! I can't see anybody!'

'That's not the point, Whacker! Just because we can't see them doesn't mean there's nobody to see us. I've not spent all this time on THE PLAN for you to blow it before we've even started!' Slim always thought of The Plan in capital letters, but he wasn't sure that the others did; Whacker certainly didn't, but Boots might – he was much more responsible.

But even Boots seemed to be on Whacker's side at the moment. 'Ease up a bit, Slim. It's not the end of the world if we're spotted now; they'll know we're here when we book in at the pub.'

'For the last time, you two, it's not a PUB it's an INN!' Slim almost allowed his voice to rise in his exasperation. 'Anyway, when we're booking in we'll be on their territory and they won't want to cause a scene in front of other customers, even if they think they have good cause. And you two,' though Slim looked only at Whacker, 'are the only ones that might give them cause. So, smarten up and try to look as though you have every right to be here!'

Anyone seeing the three of them together would know which one was called Slim, because he was. Slim, that is. Slim Bennett had slim hips and narrow shoulders that led up to a narrow head, and his slightly protruding teeth could give the impression that his head had been squashed slightly flat, side to side. So, top to toe, he was just slim. And he was neat in looks and in thoughts and actions. The first time he did anything, no matter how small, he'd look at what was involved and work out the most efficient way to do it; if he was satisfied with the effort and time it took, he'd always do it that way – and irritate the hell out of anybody being more relaxed about doing the same thing!

Not surprisingly, his attitude applied to his learning to play the guitar. He had a reasonable singing voice and decided that accompanying himself on the guitar would be more efficient than belonging to a choir. His mother encouraged him and wasn't surprised at how scales and chord structures fascinated him and satisfied his interest. But she was very surprised when he started spending time with a very relaxed lad called, of all things, Whacker.

She wasn't the only one surprised by this new friendship. After all, Whacker Bailey was a year junior to Slim and was his antithesis in almost every way, but not in his attitude to music. Whacker was an amiable lad who seemed to shamble through life, but if you put drumsticks in his hands he came to life producing steady rhythms and the occasional simple riff that supported and complemented Slim's chords. But this was really all that kept this tentative friendship afloat. In all things but their music, Slim was irritated by almost everything about Whacker.

It was anyone's guess how long this 'friendship' would last; but then it was augmented and cemented by the arrival of Boots Clark who seemed to bridge all the gaps between Slim and Whacker. Boots' identifiable contribution to the pair was his flair with words – he was less brusque than Slim could be, and more articulate than Whacker sometimes was – but, when it came to song lyrics, they could flow like honey from a jar. Furthermore, as a contemporary of Slim's, he was approved of by Mrs Bennett, Slim's mum.

In addition to their music, the lads found they shared an interest in the countryside. This came to light when they found they all enjoyed taking the long way home from school via paths away from the road network. This soon led to taking walks in nearby parks, and then they were backpacking for whole weekends. It was on one of these that turned cold and wet in some remote woods, that one of them – and they could never remember who – said he'd rather be staying bed and breakfast in Charlford.

And so, the weekend was planned – by Slim, of course – with the slight worry that they might be seen simply as a gang of youths intent on getting up to some sort of mischief. Hence the plan required them to travel slightly separately and to try to look respectable. Slim always worried about their combined appearance and what impression they made on people. Even in T-shirts and jeans, as they were now, Slim was ultra-smart – if they'd worn shoes instead of trainers, his would have had a mirror shine. Boots was, as always, comfortably casual. Whacker, also as always, was casual bordering on the scruffy; if T-shirts had buttons, his would be missing. Even so, their personal appearances would have alarmed no-one, though their luggage hinted at their intentions.

As they waited at the end of the path, ready to enter the village, it was Whacker who broke the silence. 'What's the difference between a kilo of lard and square peg in a round hole?' Slim rounded on him with a glare while Boots spluttered and dropped his backpack. Before Slim could vent his annoyance, Boots came to the rescue with the expected response – 'I don't know, what is the difference?'

'One's a good lot of fat and the other's a fat lot of good!'

This earned a good laugh from Boots, but the joke didn't register with Slim. 'For Pete's sake, Whacker, don't come out with anything like that in the village or you'll have us thrown out. Anyway, where do you get that puerile stuff from?'

'A book of jokes in the library, and not the kiddies' section either, so it's not puerile!' Whacker occasionally liked to show he wasn't ignorant – but not too often in case Slim realised how bright he was and gave him more jobs to do.

Slim didn't believe Whacker about the origin of the joke, but didn't want to argue. Away from their music, he didn't argue, and rarely discussed things with the Whackers of this world; they shouldn't have opinions, they should just do as they were told and not be a pain. The fact that Whacker knew at least one big word – puerile – didn't make him less ignorant, not in Slim's estimation, anyway.

Fortunately for all concerned the situation was brought to an end by the bus coming into view and slowing down for the nearby stop. They pulled back into the shade as it trundled past, then they picked up their assorted baggage and moved forward quickly to mingle with the emerging passengers – some tired at the end of the week, others excited at the start of the weekend. They were of various ages and mainly knew each other, chatting, calling 'cheerio', and making their ways home. But two of them, a middle-aged couple with suitcases, seemed to be strangers who paused to get their bearings. As the bus pulled away in a cloud of exhaust fumes, the couple found they were now part of a group of five, having been joined by the three lads looking for all the world as if they, too, had just got off the bus.

Slim was quick to reinforce that impression. 'What a journey! You'd think a service as well used as this would deserve a newer bus, wouldn't you? Never mind, soon be settled in. Are you at the Red Lion as well?' The man could barely nod before Slim went on, 'Fine. Let's give you a hand with your luggage.'

And that was how the three, luckier than they'd dared hope, entered the Red Lion in the company of a respectable-looking couple and, by association, were accepted as bona fide visitors – at least for a start.

Slim had worried about this part of The Plan, after their experiences when they'd dropped in at the Red Lion on earlier backpacking weekends. They'd found it to be just what you'd expect of an English country inn – floors either carpeted or of polished wood, the walls displaying country-side pictures and artefacts, with polished brass here and there. All this, and a roaring log fire when they visited last October, had made it seem like Heaven on earth.

Now, things changed at reception when the couple, Mr and Mrs Wilkinson, had booked in and moved off to find their room, and the receptionist turned to find the lads still there. 'Right, lads, what can we do for you? The bar's that way and the beer garden is just off it.'

'We want to book in,' said Slim.

'Sorry, but we're full, and anyway we don't take groups of all males,' and she turned to walk back into the office.

'But we've got rooms booked for the weekend,' said Slim. 'Booked and paid for!'

'Our agent phoned and booked,' interceded Boots, 'and sent a cheque to cover the weekend.'

'Hello, I'm Sarah Bennett. I'm representing a new band – The Acolytes – looking to spend a couple of nights in Charlford. It's part of the final preparations for their up-coming tour. I wonder if you could help? ...No, not a big band, just the three of them and all they want is a bed for a couple of nights ...yes, a couple of attic rooms would be fine ... it's all acoustic stuff so they don't have amps... they don't make too much noise and they'll mainly be out and about in the woods and fields...but if the weather is bad they'd want to be able to practise somewhere under cover, perhaps a garage or outhouse.... – Thank you very much.'

'I'll have a word with the landlord,' and disappeared.

'So much for THE PLAN, Slim,' said Boots. 'Are you sure your mum phoned the right place or sent the cheque?' Seeing Slim was taking it hard, he eased off and followed up with, 'Easy to do that with a common name like The Red Lion.'

Before Slim could respond, the girl was back with the landlord in tow. Not quite your genial-looking 'mine host', but equally not glowering. His black polo shirt, with 'Red Lion Charlford' embroidered on it, displayed muscular forearms like you see on many a golfer but, in his case, probably due to handling barrels of beer. Definitely not someone to get on the wrong side of.

'Now then, lads, what's the problem... *and*, one at a time please!'

Before Boots could take over again, Slim jumped in, 'You had a phone call on the 3rd asking for rooms for us, The Acolytes, for three nights starting tonight and you were sent a cheque to cover B and B. Call was from Sarah Bennett who also sent the cheque. Your receptionist can't seem to find it.'

'Slow down a minute,' said the landlord, 'the booking is in order, we just need to check that you are indeed the people it was made – and paid – for. So, if you can give me the phone number Mrs Bennett rang from and a piece of ID for one of you, we'll be happy.'

Slim rattled off his home number and Boots flashed his library membership card, and everybody looked relieved when the landlord gave the receptionist the nod and moved off, probably back to the bar.

The receptionist handed over the keys to adjoining rooms on the top floor and Slim immediately bagged the single on the basis that he'd organised it and – to himself – because he didn't need Whacker or Boots chatting at him all the time – Boots was OK but Whacker could be a bit childish at times.

He unpacked, then stuck his head in their door. 'Come on you two, let's get out to the field for a practice before we find something to eat.'

'I'm with you,' said Boots.

'I'll catch you up,' said Whacker. 'I need the bog first.'

'Thank Heaven for that,' said Boots as he and Slim went downstairs, 'perhaps the air will have cleared by the time we get back.'

CHAPTER 2

Taking their guitars and the well-known route to the edge of the village, Slim and Boots were soon leaning on the handrail of the footbridge gazing into the shallow and slow-moving waters of the river Charl where it flowed over the ford that gave the village its name.

'Great to be here again, Boots… can't think why we've not done it before.'

'Cash, Slim me old mate! None of us has got enough, and Heaven knows when we'll be earning enough, or even earning at all! Just got to make the most of it this time.'

'Yeah, you're right. Let's get on down to the field and hope ruddy Whacker gets a move on.'

Soon they were over a stile and into a meadow filled with lovely soft hay that they assumed had been laid out to dry, and was certainly doing so in the evening sun. They couldn't help having a kick around and a good roll in it, hoping that Whacker wouldn't arrive too soon when they'd have to calm down ready for their first run-through of the weekend.

The aim was to polish up their latest two songs and try out a couple more Mystic Wizards' pieces but, before they could start, they were interrupted by the giggly arrival of a quartet of teenage girls.

Both groups stopped in surprise and no-one spoke for the best part of a minute then the tallest of the girls, Anna, called out – 'Hey, you two, what do you think you're doing here?'

Boots was quickest to reply, 'We know what we're doing, thanks – how about you lot?' with a grin to take the edge off.

'Well, we're not trespassing, for a start,' was the quick reply from the same girl.

'How do you mean, trespassing?' asked Boots. 'It's a public footpath through here, the sign says so.'

'And it's right, but the path runs *around* the edge and is only the width of a path, NOT the width of the field!'

'So, who are you, the local copper?'

'No,' said Anna, 'but my dad owns the field, so either use the path or leave the field altogether, you're damaging the crop!'

Just then Whacker arrived and obviously hadn't heard any of the exchange, judging by his opening remark – 'What's this then, found some backing vocals?'

'Who's this, another trespasser?' asked Anna. 'And what's this about backing vocals? Don't try and tell us you're a chart-topping band in hiding!!' and she and the other girls burst into a fit of giggles again.

'Not yet, but we're a chart-topping band in the making, and you're getting in the way of some serious rehearsals,' Slim replied. 'Come on lads, let's move on a bit and find a quiet corner.'

The girls stopped giggling and Anna, the obvious leader, said, 'Don't be mardy, let's hear what you do – my dad won't mind, if I say it's OK for you to stay for a bit.'

After some chat, the lads decided to stay and, after some more chat, settled on one of their own pieces to play.

'OK,' said Whacker, 'this is "Autumn Morning" by The Acolytes – first public performance after not enough rehearsal! OK lads – Tractor one, tractor two…'

And the intro was there, just as written! Lost in concentration the lads played and sang as never before, forgetting the audience, remembering only the inspiration for the song – and it showed! The girls were silent until the last chord had died and then they burst into excited applause and acclaim.

'Wow! Where did that come from? I mean, did you really write it, and who did the words and who did the music? And what was it called again?'

'It's called "Autumn Morning" and we wrote it,' said Slim. 'Not sure now where the initial idea came from, but we all joined in with the words then Boots tidied them up, then Boots and me rounded off the music. That's usually how it goes, anyway, so that's why we say it's by The Acolytes.'

'And what's that tractor thing at the start?'

'Whacker's the drummer so he always counts us in – you tell it Whacker.'

'Well it came from the Mystic Wizards. As a sort of private venture, Apoth wrote a play about a band and the drummer counted them in with, "Tractor one, tractor two..." and so on, so it was a Tractor Countdown – and Apoth went on to do a lot of stuff under that name, so it all links up, sort of.'

The girls looked absolutely lost and didn't seem to know which question to ask first!

'Sorry, but what on earth are you talking about?' asked Debs, the smallest of the girls. 'Mystic Wizards? A *poth*? What on earth is a poth?'

'It's a bit too much to go into just now,' said Slim, 'but the Mystic Wizards is, or was, a band we look up to, sort of base ourselves on. They used mystic names like Apoth, short for Apothecary, and Card for Cardinal, and Speed – not sure where that came from. Anyway, as I say, we like to follow them and base ourselves on them. Hence our name, The Acolytes, and that's why we're here, at Charlford, as near as we can get to Charlbury, the Wizards' spiritual home.'

'But acolytes are servers in Church, not pop groups!' exclaimed Belinda – Bel for short.

'But they are also followers, and that's what we are – followers of the Mystic Wizards.'

'Who nobody's ever heard of!!'

'But they'll get to know all about them when we hit the stage big time,' said Slim.

'And what stage will that be? Some barn you've broken into, no doubt!' said Clare, the girl who hadn't spoken before. 'Come on, girls, let's move on, we've wasted enough time here!'

'Wait a mo,' said Anna, 'that was good and I wouldn't mind hearing a bit more. Will you play another one, lads?'

'Hang on a minute, are we supposed to get off your dad's land, or stay and play? Make your mind up,' said Slim, growing impatient.

'I don't see any lipstick on her forehead,' observed Whacker.

'What on earth are you on about, Whacker?' demanded Slim.

'Trying to "make up" her mind – make up – get it?' explained Whacker, again getting a chuckle from Boots, but puzzled looks from those girls that had heard him.

'I'd really like to hear another one,' said Anna, getting them back to business, 'and, if it's as good as "Autumn Morning", I have an idea that might work out good for us all.'

'OK, we'll do one of the Mystic Wizards' pieces – "Charlbury Moon", lads?'

With the appropriate countdown, the boys launched into what many of their followers consider to be the ultimate Mystic Wizards number, identifying landmarks and recreating the atmosphere of earlier Charlbury days. But the song ended to muted applause.

'Didn't you like it, then?' asked Slim.

'Well, yes, but what's all this about Charlbury? The place is miles away!'

'Oh, that's too much to go into right now. Just tell us what this good idea is that you've got for us, and if we agree we can tell you more about the Wizards.'

Anna went into a huddle with the other girls and all that the lads could hear were giggles, shushes, OK's and finally, 'But what about your dad?'

'Right,' said Anna, turning to the lads, 'here's the idea; we're having a party tomorrow for my birthday and Dad's got a DJ guy coming for it. BUT, before it starts when we're having a bite to eat, Dad will probably put on some of his own CDs and that will be AWFUL. So, we think it would be cool to have a real live band – you – instead! What do you think?'

The lads didn't know what to think. They'd only done a couple of gigs, one in Slim's back garden for a couple of mates and one at school for Boots' class – neither had been the success they'd expected or hoped for. They didn't admit it, even amongst themselves but, while they each liked the idea of being famous, they weren't sure they fancied the work that went into getting there – and they certainly didn't want to run the risk of facing a rejection so soon.

So, they had the problem of how to get out of doing the gig without losing face. Slim, as ever, had the solution – 'Whacker hasn't got his drums, so we can't – sorry!'

'No problem,' said Anna, 'my dad's got a set.'

'Your dad's a drummer?' almost squawked Whacker, seeing a chance for some tips and tuition.

'No, course he's not!!' laughed Anna. 'Soft devil took them in for a bad debt, but he was the one that got taken in – nobody wants to buy them from him!'

'Best go and give 'em a try, Whacker,' said Slim, unusually happy to put off a decision – and to let someone else take the blame!

'Go back over the stile, turn left, and follow the path round the wood till you get to a gate on the right. Go through – and mind you close the gate after you! – and you can't miss the Manor House on your left. You'll find my dad somewhere round there.' ('Lord of the Manor,' giggled Debs, almost under her breath.) 'Ease up, Debs, you know he's not like that.'

Following Anna's directions, Whacker set off wondering what to expect of the drums and how to deal with them. He fully understood and agreed with Slim's unspoken intention that a duff set of drums would provide the perfect opt-out. But, was that what the band really wanted? For the first time, they'd found an appreciative audience. These girls obviously enjoyed the pieces, so they only had to repeat them with a couple more in the middle and, who knows, fame might be around the corner and easier to deal with than they'd expected. Unbeknown to Whacker, both Slim and Boots were having very similar thoughts and hoping that the drums would be good and thus force them to play at the party.

Chapter 3

At Whacker's destination, Anna's dad, Tony Philips, was leaning against the gate – it marked the end of the road that ran past the Manor House, and he felt it could equally mark the end of his hopes for living there. Gazing over the nearest couple of fields, he was lost in thought. What to do now? Had it all gone wrong? If not, what to do now? If it had gone wrong, it was still a question of what to do now! Talk it over with Anna? Or was she too young to be burdened with such things? It all came down to what to do now, and he didn't even know whom he could discuss it with.

This never-ending reverie of worry and self-doubt was interrupted by Whacker's arrival. 'Scuse me, I'm looking for the lord of the manor – have you seen him?' he asked.

This immediately lifted Tony's spirits and he replied as anyone who knew him would have expected. 'Not since first thing this morning, sorry.' Then, seeing Whacker's puzzled expression, 'What did you need him for? Can I help at all?'

'Not sure, really. His daughter, or at least a girl who says she's his daughter, says he's got some drums I can look at. Do you know anything about them?'

Resisting the temptation to ask if he wanted oil drums or eardrums, Tony decided to come clean. 'If she's a tallish girl with blond hair, that's my daughter Anna. And yes, this is my place – Charlford Manor – and some of her friends like to call me the lord of the manor, but I'm not.'

'So, I don't address you as Milord, then?'

'No, you don't, my lad! Mr Philips will do. Anyway, what's this about the drums? Are you looking to buy some?'

'Not unless they're dirt cheap! No, she wants us to play at her party tomorrow, but we can't unless I can get hold of a drum – just a snare would do and some brushes if you've got some.'

'Let's go and have a look, and you'd best tell me who you are and what's this about playing at her party.'

'Well, we're a band called The Acolytes – just three of us – and she, your daughter, liked a couple of pieces we did for her and her friends out in the hay field – you know, the one near the ford. She just wants us to play a short set while they're eating. If it's a small venue we won't need any power – we're all acoustic – so the drum's the only problem.'

'No, son, there's at least one more problem – me and the disco guy. I've booked him for the evening and he wants to be paid for that – fair enough?' Whacker nodded. 'On top of that, you're asking me to pay you for time I've already paid somebody else for. You're not looking at a bottomless pit of money you know. Just because somebody's got a big house, it doesn't mean they've got money – it means they *had* money, but now they're probably facing bigger bills than they expected.'

Tony stopped, suddenly realising he'd said more to this stranger than he had to anyone else about his financial concerns.

An awkward silence was broken by Whacker. 'Sorry, I should have explained – we're not asking for payment, it's really just a rehearsal with an audience, if that's good enough for you. I think your daughter understands that.'

'It's OK, lad,' sighed Tony, 'it's me that should apologise for going off at you like that. Only I'm trying to sort things out in my head – and I should have kept it there. Let's go see these drums!' And he led off with a smile, feeling a bit more relaxed, probably simply because he'd voiced his thoughts – or at least some of them.

These thoughts went back three years or more to when things began to feel not quite right between himself and his wife. After much pondering, he'd decided that his wife was probably cheating on him, but he didn't know how to deal with it. For Annabel's sake, they referred to it as a rocky patch in their marriage. Annabel was at that very awkward age, twelve and a bit, and was starting to really need a mum and friend, but her mum seemed to have found a new friend – perhaps more than a friend – elsewhere. After much soul-searching, it was decided that Annabel should go to boarding school where she would hopefully develop close friendships and have the support of the school staff while he and his wife sorted out their problems – if they *could* be sorted.

Once Annabel was away at school they found it easier to talk openly and his wife very soon admitted she was seeing someone else, that it was serious, and that she wanted a divorce. While this stunned him, it soon dawned on him that he wasn't too bothered! On the positive side, his haulage and scrap metal business was thriving, even expanding a bit. While it was great to have a wife and family to come home to every day, he and his wife shared no real interests outside his work – except for the safety and security of Annabel, the real light of his life.

Over the past few months he had begun to notice that he was putting on a bit of weight, then realised that his wife was bringing home much better cuts of meat, and cooking it beautifully. So, it should have been no big surprise when she told him that the other man was a butcher – except for the fact that his wife used to profess to be a vegetarian!!

A big plus about the situation, as far as Tony was concerned, was that the 'other' chap – he could never bring himself to refer to the chap by name – wanted only a wife, not a wife complete with teenage daughter. And Tony's wife was so wrapped up in the idea of a new life that she was happy for Annabel to be in the care of her dad, as she knew he doted on her. In spite of all her activity behind his back, Tony was still fond of his wife and decided that, if the other chap could make her happier than he could, he wouldn't stand in her way.

He'd already worked out that he would need to sell up the house, and perhaps even the business, to pay whatever the divorce court awarded his wife, so why not have a complete break, move away, and make fresh beginnings. This should also be acceptable to Annabel, particularly during school holidays. Being at boarding school meant that she'd largely lost real contact with her old friends from around where they lived. This situation was made worse by the fact that she now insisted on being called Anna – her best friend at boarding school was called Bel (*work it out*) – and most of her former friends thought she'd gone all stuck up since going to boarding school.

The divorce was granted quite quickly and the other bloke being, in Tony's mind, a bit of a pompous git, he didn't want his new life demeaned by any money from Tony's house or business – particularly a scrap metal business. But the house sale was going through and Tony's business partner, Reg Harris, was ready to buy up most of Tony's share of the business, so he let both deals proceed while he looked for a suitable new home 'with potential' – as the agents liked to describe such things.

When the Manor House in Charlford was brought to his attention, at what seemed a very reasonable price, Tony jumped at it. Nice house, lovely village, a bit of land to 'do things' with, stables for Anna to take up riding – just the job! He was now wondering if his planning had been thorough enough.

But back to the present, getting rid of that wretched set of drums would be a small step in the right direction, he decided, and led Whacker through a pair of tall gates set in the near end of the high wall that ran away along the side of the road.

'Right,' he said, 'this is what I call the stable yard.'

Yup, thought Whacker, a good name for a yard with stables in it! What on earth am I dealing with here? Should there be blokes in white coats keeping an eye on him? But, of course, he said nothing.

Then, pointing to the wall across the yard from the stables, Tony went on, 'But I'm reliably informed that the yard up there – between that wall and the Manor House – is what was called the service yard.'

Seeing Whacker's slightly puzzled expression, Tony explained, 'I reckon you can tell I've not lived here very long – I haven't even looked in all these places yet.' He swept his arm around to indicate the brick buildings facing each other across the width of the cobbled yard. 'Anyway, I'm using names for the yards to try to get the layout fixed in my mind, and it helps when I need to describe locations to people..... and I really must try and find a key to that one,' pointing to the smallish brick building standing in the top right-hand corner of the yard, 'but at least I know where the drum kit is – I'm pretty sure.'

Feeling happier about the situation, Whacker followed Tony up the yard, away from the stables, passing pairs of very tall, very wide, doors of what he guessed had been coach houses. Reaching the last of them, Tony pulled open the right-hand door, saying, 'Right, lad, this is where we start looking.'

'Gosh!' said Whacker. 'What's all this, then?' looking at the mounds covered by dust sheets, old blankets and rugs.

'Some stuff from my old house, some from the main house here, and just a few bits from the cottage over there – all waiting for decisions.'

'And is that drum kit in here somewhere?'

'Yes, and I'm just trying to think where.... it wasn't in the first lot from the old house – I left it handy there in case anybody wanted it before I finally left. So, yeah, it must be somewhere behind these nearest lots – these are mainly what I brought in from the main house to get it clear of the work being done in there – and I'm still not sure if I want to put it back.'

'Don't want to be nosey,' interrupted Whacker, 'but if you've sold your old house and emptied the Manor House while work is being done in there, where are you living? Sorry, shouldn't ask. None of my business.'

'No problem, and you're not the first to ask. No, we're living in the cottage over there,' pointing to the two-storey building that now faced them, a few yards down from the little building in the corner. 'At least, we *were* both living in there, Anna and me, but as soon as she knew her pals were coming for the birthday weekend she got me to organise some beds for them all in the rooms over the stables – they think it's great. It's a bit too Spartan for me, but it gives me the cottage to myself for a while. Anyway, we were looking for the drums.'

'Yes, sorry. How do you want to tackle it?'

'Well, we can't put stuff in the walkway down the side as I still need to be able to get to things at the back, so we'd best move stuff next door. Let's make sure there's a space for it, OK?'

As they moved out to the door of the adjacent coach house, Whacker asked, 'Have you got more of the same in here, then?'

'No, I've not looked in yet, but I assume it's empty, apart from spiders and such, like the first one was. Here goes.' He undid the lock, opened the door and exclaimed, 'Blow me!' For there, filling the space, was an enclosed carriage ready for a pair of horses to be hitched up to the shafts.

For a full minute, the pair of them stood looking, first at the carriage and then at each other, then they both started speaking at the same time.

'What's that doing here?' – Tony

'I thought you said it was empty.' – Whacker.

'I've not looked in here before and I just assumed it was empty – the first one was, and there was nothing listed as being in here, and I'm sure the solicitor would have noticed and mentioned if a carriage was listed anywhere in the paperwork,' all in one breath!

'So, is it really yours, then – to keep, I mean?' asked Whacker, eagerly hoping it was.

'Need to check with the solicitor, but I reckon it is – I seem to recall him saying the whole estate was now mine "lock, stock and barrel" and I can't imagine that that excludes ruddy horse-drawn carriages!!'

'What a find!'

'And what's that you've found, Whacker?' asked Slim, arriving with Boots and the girls.

'Only a stagecoach that nobody knew about! I mean, how can you not tell somebody there's a real live stagecoach in a building you're selling?'

'What's it all about, Dad?' asked Anna. 'Another of your weird surprises for my birthday? And how did you get it here without anybody knowing and not telling me?'

'Hang on a minute, love. What the young chap said is right – this is the first time I've laid eyes on it, but I'm not sure it's what you'd call a stagecoach. And honestly, I knew nothing about it – I've not opened this door before, I'm just looking for space to move things out of next door so we can get at that drum kit.'

Everybody was in the space now, looking at the carriage, touching the wheels and the bits of bodywork that they could reach. It was dusty, with lots of spiders' webs, and these put the girls off getting too close, but Whacker couldn't get close enough.

'What's the fascination then, young man?' asked Tony. 'You're not a secret carriage driver, are you?' and laughed.

'No, it's the woodwork, I suppose what you'd call the bodywork. My dad's a cabinetmaker and he likes to study old items to see if he can find any long-lost tricks of the trade.'

'Well, give him a ring and he can come and have a look while we're moving stuff – better still, he can give us a hand!'

'Not as easy as that with us living in Bracknell,' said Whacker, 'plus he'll be taking my mum out shopping, then probably out for the day tomorrow while I'm not hangin' around needing to be fed!'

'Well that's OK – any time he can come over would be fine. He can perhaps give me some idea of its quality so I can work out what it's worth. For now, folks, let's get to this drum kit and see if we've found a taker for it.'

They all got stuck in, moving chairs, settees, tables, a sideboard, things they couldn't identify, and a couple of rolls of carpet, the latter setting them off in coughing fits from the clouds of dust they created. Then, at last, the drum kit came into view – not the full sparkling kit that Whacker had in mind but a jumble of stands, pedals, cymbals, a bass drum and two or three smaller ones.

'Right, lad, what do you think of it? Is it something you could use?' asked Tony.

'Not really sure,' said Whacker, looking as downcast as he felt. 'I'd need to get it cleaned up a bit and see what state all the bits are in. But if it's all OK, I'm sorry but it would be more than I could afford, and I'm not sure where it could go at home.'

'Don't worry about the money, lad. If you could make good use of them I'd be glad to let them go. As you can see, I've got more than enough stuff to decide what to do with. They're probably too good to be just dumped, and if they stayed in here, Heaven knows what state they'd get in. Why don't you have a word with your dad about the carriage, and when he comes to have a look you can talk to him about the drums – that is, if they're worth doing anything with.'

'That's really great, Mr Philips. I'll give him a ring when we're finished – he'll likely be at home this evening.'

Chapter 4

The lads joined Tony in moving the drum bits and pieces out into the yard, but the girls gave up any pretence of helping and disappeared towards the house.

Tony wanted to put everything back into the first storage bay so as to leave the carriage on its own again while he decided what to do with it – assuming it really was his to do with as he pleased. But first he felt he ought to know a bit more about Whacker and his mates.

'Now then, lads,' he said. 'I can't keep calling you just "lads", so how about some introductions – you know who I am, Tony Philips, so who are you?'

'Well,' jumped in Slim, 'I'm known as Slim and I'm the sort of driving force of our band, The Acolytes. We're followers of the Mystic Wizards and our work is strongly influenced by theirs – when we perform one of their numbers and then one of our own, most people wouldn't know who had written which of them.'

'And this is Boots,' continued Slim. 'He's the real wordsmith and not bad with a melody either – in fact we're complementary in the creative department, a modern-day Lennon and McCartney or, for those who knew the Wizards, a new Apoth and Cardinal. Young Whacker here is our rhythm and doesn't offer much in the writing department, but that's OK – I suppose you'd call him our Speed – I don't think that Speed did much creative stuff, but I could be wrong – in fact I'd better check on that.'

Fortunately for Slim, he couldn't see Whacker who was doubled up and almost helpless trying not to laugh. When Slim was spouting this pretentious drivel, as Whacker considered it to be, it had the same effect on anyone who knew the band. In Whacker's opinion, they were just a gang of mates that liked to have a go at writing and performing. As far as Slim was concerned, they were destined for success sooner or later – and probably sooner if Whacker wasn't such a liability!

'Hold your horses a bit,' said Tony. 'This may be all very well in your music world, but I live in the real world. I don't mind calling you two Slim and Boots, but Whacker sounds too much like wacky – you know, nutty, a bit of a nut case – and I'm sure he's not, are you, lad?' addressing Whacker.

'I'm OK with Whacker, in fact only my mum uses my real name.'

'OK, then. A bit more about yourselves, if you don't mind – after all, I am letting you in my house on trust.'

Boots started it off. 'I'm about to start my last year before going to college for art, design, English literature – somewhere in that area depending on my A level results and how the different threads develop. This weekend is a bit of a final fling while we're all together. We've been backpacking in various areas, but really like it round here. Staying B&B at the Red Lion is a bit of a treat.'

'You know a bit about me already,' said Whacker. 'I'm into wood, like my dad, and waiting to hear if I could get an apprenticeship in cabinetmaking. If not, I guess I'll stay on at school and see if the design side develops.'

'What about you, then, Slim? And not about the music again, please.'

Slim looked quite a bit put out at this but rallied round and addressed the request. 'Well I'm getting ready for interviews to join the Police!' and he really did say it with a capital P and an exclamation mark at the end.

'Good for you, all of you. Nice to come across three young chaps with honest plans for the future. Pleased to meet you all.' And he shook each of them by the hand, much to their surprise.

'Now, if there's time when we finish here I'd like to ask you all a favour. Not you, though, Whacker. You grab some of those old sheets or towels and have a go at cleaning up the drums. Take them over to the end stable, the one next to where we came in the yard – you'll find a key in the padlock – and you can leave the lot in there when you've finished.

'I'll do what I can with this side drum, 'cos that's all I'll need for now, but I'd need proper tools and such to do the job properly on all of them. Anyway, thanks for letting me have a go and I'll be as quick as I can.'

But as he peeled off to the stables, Whacker grabbed – yes, actually grabbed – Slim's arm to get his attention, before whispering, none too quietly, 'No need to check about Speed's contribution to the Wizards, mate, he did the words for "Charlbury Moon"! And you know how good that is! So don't go putting him down, OK?'

This almost 'outburst' – never before having been grabbed by the arm like that, and certainly never having been addressed as 'mate' – left Slim somewhat bewildered, and it took a moment for him to catch up and join in with Boots and Tony. Under Tony's guidance they were moving the odds and ends back into the first coach house, with the result that it all ended up a lot tidier and took up less space. At last, only the carriage remained, on its own, as it had been found.

They were about to close the door on it when Boots spotted a rope, coiled on the floor under the front of the carriage. 'Don't forget the rope,' he said, pointing.

'That's not one of mine,' said Tony. 'Never saw it before – didn't spot it when we were all staring at the carriage – best leave it until it all gets sorted out.' So, they carried on and closed the door, putting the carriage out of sight but not out of mind.

'Now, lads, if you'll come with me into the house I'll show you where I think you'd be best placed if you play tomorrow evening, and you can give me a sample of what you'd play, if you're ready. After that I'd appreciate a bit of a hand with a few tables I want to get in from the summerhouse – I've just realised they need to be here ready for when the caterers turn up tomorrow.'

Slim's face fell. This situation had all the hallmarks of them being used as free labour with the guy having no intention of even giving them an audition, let alone a gig. But seeing the look of dismay on Slim's face, Tony added, 'Sorry to be a bit pushy, but if you're booked in at the inn for a meal I'll give them a ring and get them to put it back a bit.

And don't forget, if I'd not spent time looking for the drum kit for you I'd not be running late.' He wasn't too happy about making that last point as he'd only just thought about it when he realised he needed to move the tables – he had, after all, quite enjoyed their company.

Slim was really keen on the opportunity to perform here so he brushed aside Tony's worries. 'We don't know yet what we're doing for a meal, so show us where we can play and we can do a demo that'll also check the acoustics,' he said, before Boots could express his own views.

Tony set off towards the gate into the service yard then paused and called over to where Whacker was just closing the stable door. 'Everything OK, lad? We're just going to see about a try-out in the house. Have you got a drum you can use?'

'Not quite,' replied Whacker, 'and I reckon it would take me another hour or so – would it be OK to come back to do more tomorrow morning?'

'Of course, and you can do that whether you're coming to play later, or not. I did mean it about you having those drums if you can make something of them.'

Slim could hardly believe his ears. Here was Whacker, the slob, or was it yob, of the band, getting access to a full drum kit just for the asking! And it didn't seem as if he'd actually asked for it, apart from to borrow it! After all the work that he, Slim, put into the band it just wasn't fair! He actually felt like crying, but managed to pull himself together for the sake of the Acolytes – his time would come with, or without, Whacker and his drum!!

Tony led them into the house through one of the two doors set in the back wall of the Manor House; it led into a corridor that had doors to a couple of rooms – one looked like a kitchen, while the other could have been a work room or store. At the far end of the corridor was a door that Tony opened for them all to go into the main reception hall of the house.

'Right, lads, while we get the tables and chairs in you can be looking to see where you'd like to be stationed for your set – that's the right word, yeah? The disco chap will be in that far corner of the room on the right, the lounge or sitting room or whatever it's supposed to be called. He's booked to give us background music while people are eating before getting on with the stuff to jig around to.'

Like the house overall, the reception hall was a good size but not grand in either proportions or appearance. There was the wide main entrance door, and a staircase that ran up two sides of the hall. The middle of the tiled floor was covered by a large square of dusty-looking carpet, and the walls carried a few old-looking portraits and landscape paintings and a few tapestries here and there, but the general feel of the place was not of real history.

Just lately, Tony had spent a lot of time wondering if he'd been far too quick in buying the place. He felt sure he'd got the best price for his house and business, but had he been wise in buying this Manor House? The surveyors and valuers agreed it was a sound buy, but that wasn't the problem. The real problem – well, there were at least two of them – so the main problem was that he realised he could soon become bored when all the remedial and updating work was finished. It can look and sound very nice to live in a big house on the edge of a pretty country village, but – and he now knew it was a big 'but' – what do you do with yourself all day, every day??

This weekend celebrating Anna's sixteenth birthday was just what he needed to occupy him, and having these three lads to talk to was quite a bonus – as long as he remembered that they were just lads, with little worldly experience.

They all got stuck into moving tables and chairs from the summerhouse into the main hall and, when he felt there were enough, he asked the lads how they felt about doing a demo, but they all declined, having got quite dusty/dirty from their recent labours. So Tony insisted that they took some money for their suppers then waved them off.

'Come along some time in the morning, lads, then we can have a run-through so I'll be able to decide what we might want to do, and we'll see how it fits in the time before the disco chap turns up.'

With that the lads set off back to the village with their guitars, drum sticks, money for supper and heads full of dreams that they could be on the verge of a breakthrough into a career in music, perhaps the first step on the stairway to stardom!

Chapter 5

After dropping their instruments in their rooms and having a quick (read 'very quick') wash, the lads went out onto the village green where the Fish and Chip van was doing a steady trade, rather to the annoyance of the landlord of the Red Lion. The pub did good meals that were reasonably priced, but on a warm summer evening you couldn't beat freshly cooked fish and chips outside, chatting with your mates and eyeing up the talent, both male and female.

This was just what the lads fancied, particularly after the hot dusty work at the Manor House, and it was a chance to relax and share the dream of a proper gig and what it might lead to. Slim, as ever, was taking it seriously and they'd barely finished their fish and chips when he got them thinking about what to offer in the set. Obviously, they'd do 'Autumn Morning', as the girls had really liked it, but save it for the end.

'I reckon we should open with a Wizards' number such as "Charlbury Moon", right?' said Boots. 'Then, what about "Sunshine Calling" and finish with "Autumn Morning".'

'Do you think that'll be enough?' asked Slim.

'Could be more than enough,' replied Whacker. 'Surely, it's best to have them ask for more – so how about we start with "Autumn Morning", we know the girls liked that, then on to a Wizards piece, but have a couple more in mind as encores?'

And so started a typical Acolytes debate that Slim resolved by going off to get a notepad. The other two looked at each other, shrugged, rolled their eyes and burst out laughing – you had to laugh when Slim was in manager mode!

'You two look nice and relaxed and happy.' It was Mrs W, the lady who'd innocently helped them make their entrance to the Red Lion. 'What's the matter with your friend? We just saw him going into the inn looking really serious. Nothing wrong I hope.'

'No, everything's fine, in fact it couldn't be better. Looks like we've got ourselves a gig over the weekend down at the Manor House – Slim's just off to plan what we're going to do, and he takes it very seriously!'

Mr W had joined them while Boots was saying this, and both he and his wife looked extremely interested.

'Have you met the owners of the Manor House, then?' asked Mr W. 'I mean the new owners?'

'How would they know if they're the new owners or the previous ones, Harry?'

'Yes, we have,' replied Whacker, 'and they are – or at least *he* is – the new owner, and still settling in. It's his daughter's birthday and we're hoping to give them a song or two.'

For once, Whacker had realised in time that he shouldn't blurt out all he'd heard or been told. Mr and Mrs W seemed a nice couple, a bit like his Uncle Jim and Auntie Joan, but that didn't mean they were as nice as them or trustworthy.

Boots seemed to have the same reservations and decided to try and check them out. 'Do you know much about the Manor House, then? I mean, you knew it had been up for sale – were you hoping to buy it?'

Mr and Mrs W both seemed to realise they were being checked-up on and burst out laughing. 'I must have put my Sunday trousers on, Mary, if somebody thinks I've got the wherewithal to buy a house that size – or any house, for that matter!' And he laughed till the tears ran down his cheeks. 'Sorry, lads, not laughing at you but at the idea, really.'

Mrs W was first to calm down and carried on, 'No, we know the house because we used to work there, and we hoped to get a look at it while we're here. Just for old times' sake, really. If it'd been empty and for sale, it could have been messy trying to get an agent let us have a look. At least we now know there's a resident owner to talk to.'

'No offence taken, folks, and I'm sure Mr Philips won't mind you approaching him, but I must warn you he's going to be quite busy over the next few days. I think he's taken on more than he realises. Look, we're going down in the morning to lend him a hand, and have a bit of an audition and make final plans for the set if he says we're good enough. Why not come along with us and we can make the introduction?' Boots at his best.

'Before I forget,' said Whacker, 'I need to ring my dad about coming down. I'll just nip in and see if I can use the pub's phone – won't be a minute.'

'Can you ask if they'd bring my mum down too?' Boots called after him. 'If they can, I'll give her a ring to check it's OK with her – I reckon she'd really enjoy the run out.'

As Whacker disappeared back to the inn, 'Looks like you've been dumped, son,' chuckled Mr W, 'and we can't keep calling you son, particularly when there are three of you – and our name is Wilkinson – guess which is Mr and which isn't!' and he was off laughing fit to burst again.

Boots didn't let them see he'd noticed Mrs W give her husband a dig in the ribs to shut him up, then when he felt it safe to talk he said, 'I'm Boots – comes from our surname, Clark.' Then went on to answer the query in the raised eyebrows – 'It seems when I was quite tiny I recognised the Clark shoe shop as the place Mum took me when she was buying work boots for my dad or winter boots for herself, so every time I saw the word Clark I said "boots", and it stuck.'

'And what about the other two?'

'Well, the one that's just gone to phone his dad is Whacker – he's the drummer and has always been hitting things, hence the name. The first one you saw disappearing inside is Slim, our self-styled leader – he's alright, really, and it's good for Whacker and me to leave what you'd perhaps call the admin side of things to him 'cos he really enjoys it – but he can be a bit of a pain telling everybody that he's in charge.'

'I think I'm missing something here – er, Boots. I take it you're a musical group, but should we have heard of you? No offence meant,' said Mrs W.

'None taken. And yes, we're a band – we call ourselves The Acolytes – but we're just starting out so you won't have heard of us yet, though we hope that will change!'

Before the conversation could continue they saw and heard Whacker calling from the doorway of the inn, so they all headed that way, the Ws subconsciously not wanting to lose touch with the lads and their connection to the new owner of the Manor House.

'Boots, you see Slim chatting to that chap at the bar, well I believe he's a policeman and I reckon Slim's chatting him up for some tips on getting into the police. So, bang goes any ideas of planning for tomorrow's gig, thank goodness. Just hope he comes down to earth in time for it!'

Whacker's supposition was quite right, but Slim wasn't getting the friendly words of advice he'd expected and hoped for. Instead, his quarry, DC 'Loada' Cole, was tired at the end of a frustrating shift looking for leads in the cases of burglary that had happened over the summer in the local villages. To get rid of Slim, he'd told him the bare facts that had appeared in the local papers – that the only link between houses that had been burgled was that the occupants had been away on holidays and that none of the properties had intruder alarms. But Slim's insistent questioning elicited the fact that all the homes had at least one dog that normally would have alerted the owners to prowlers. That was all he was prepared to divulge, knowing it would be in next week's paper, and at last managed to persuade Slim to leave him in peace.

Turning from the bar and finding Boots and Whacker a pace away, Slim said, 'Right, I don't think we need an extensive set list – start with "Autumn Morning" then do others according to response – "Charlbury Moon", "Sunshine Calling", and either "Mystic Odyssey" or "The Vulture Song". I'm sure that will be enough – if not we'll decide as we go, OK?'

The others were speechless! Slim always made notes or lists! 'So, what now?' asked Boots. 'A run-through?'

'No, let's have the evening off – we don't know what tomorrow brings,' replied Whacker before Slim could get back into manager mode. 'I think something's happening in the Lounge Bar – let's go see.'

So they did, and found that the inn's Friday evening event – 'Tell-a-Tale' – was due to start. Contestants had to make up and tell a short story based on three words pulled out of three hats labelled Animal, Vegetable, and Mineral. The winner got a token to be spent in a local butcher's shop – as it was in time for Sunday dinner the event was very popular with the inn's regulars. But, on these Friday evenings in the holiday season, quite a few regulars were away, so there were only a few people ready to have a go. The landlord, Jim, really wanted to make an evening of it and was casting around for more entrants as the lads walked in.

'Now surely at least one of you lads is up for this! It doesn't cost anything and you don't have to keep the voucher if you win.' Chuckles from some of the older regulars. 'Anybody local will give you a few quid for it. So, what say, lads? If you can write a song you can surely make up a short story!'

'What's this about writing songs?' asked one of the regulars.

'They're a music group – what they call a band these days – and they're here to practise this weekend. What is it you're called, lads? At first, I thought you said "Eco Lights", and I expected you to try and sell me some fancy lighting system!!' This was greeted with much laughter from some of the older regulars, but a couple of the younger ones jumped in to the lads' defence. 'Don't listen to him. Jim, you ought to ease off, especially if you want them to join in and if you want us to stay and buy your beer!'

'Sorry, lads, don't let me put you off. Pretend we're an audience at one of your concerts.'

'They're gigs, not concerts,' shouted a youngster in the corner.

'OK, enough from you, young Harry,' raising chuckles and a few cat-calls from the locals. 'Now, anyone else going to have a go at Tell-a-Tale?' – the 'else' implying, rightly as it happened, that he'd already got one of the lads to have a go.

'Any more orders before we start?'

'Well I'll have a go at the game – if that's what you call it,' decided Boots, 'and I'll have a lemonade, please,' wondering already what on earth he'd let himself in for.

Chapter 6

The arrival of a dark cloud brought a few more punters from the Beer Garden into the Lounge Bar but none of them were prepared to show their skill, or lack of it, in storytelling, so there were just two of them ready to have a go – Boots and a local regular participant.

In the early days of holding this little entertainment, the landlord had worried about how to pick out the words for the storytellers to use – if they all used the same set, the later ones could copy bits from the first ones, but if each had a different set, it could be difficult to compare the stories. In the end, he decided that a real variety of tales was what was important, and that could only come from each participant having their own set of words, hence the separate hat for each aspect of the tale.

This evening the local guy picked out Horse, Seaweed, and Magnet, while Boots got Parrot, Apple tree, and Motorbike. As the local had done it before, he was prodded to go first and so give Boots a bit more time to think about it – and he felt he really needed that time. When writing a song, it came mainly from his own inspiration and daydreaming, so all he could think of to do here was to go out of the room while the first bloke did his stuff, and see if the words he'd drawn prompted a story line.

After about ten minutes, Boots was called back in from the Beer Garden to take his turn. He felt he was more or less ready and was encouraged by the apparent support of the younger people in the room.

'OK,' he said, 'the story started when Archie Alford got home from work on a Friday evening and found a motorbike parked up against one of the apple trees in his back garden –' at which point he was interrupted by cries from the older members of the audience to make it a proper story, cries like, 'You can't just say, "The parrot sat on the bike under the tree," and reckon that's a story, my lad!!'

'Don't fret,' Boots replied, 'you'll get your money's worth! Now, where was I? Oh yes. Archie's wife had been out shopping, so hadn't seen the bike being left there. Their garden was open to the road, so she assumed the owner had left it there after it had broken down, or something. Just before Archie got home she phoned the village bobby to report it in case it was stolen, and he asked her to get her husband to ring him when he got home, by which time he'd have an idea of how to deal with it.

'So, Archie came home, found out what had happened, then rang the Police House. He told his wife he'd been asked to hold on to the bike, lock it up and keep it safe for the time being, so that's what he did, wheeling it into the space in the back of his garage. The next day being Saturday, he spent the morning washing the car, pottering in the garage and taking a closer look at the motorbike.

'"What do you think of this, love?" he called to his wife, and showed her the two crash helmets in the panniers. "And there's what looks like a spare ignition key in with them as well. So I reckon I'd better see if she'll start up and check her out."

'His wife wasn't too happy at that but he assured her it was the best thing to do so that nobody could later accuse him of causing any problems that might have already been there. The bike had petrol and started OK so he rode it down the garden and back. "Hop on, love, and I'll give you a taste of life on a real machine" he said. He'd long hoped that his wife would at least try to get over her fear of being on only two wheels and it took a lot of persuading, but at last she agreed and they had a short run down the garden and back. He then let her off the bike and stowed it away in the garage. Later that day he said he'd forgotten to check the bike's petrol level and top it up if necessary, and again persuaded his wife to have a short ride to the bottom of the garden and back. He then rode off to the petrol station in the next village, filled the tank and rode back, beaming all over his face.'

Boots paused and took a quick drink while he marshalled his thoughts. He wanted to give an interesting story, but realised he couldn't make it too complicated or he'd lose the plot and the audience would lose patience. It didn't take too long to decide to get it over with.

'His wife met him at the gate and asked what there was to be so cheerful about. "Well," he said, "remember when you were away at your mum's and I told you I found a parrot wondering in the road, and I took it to the Police House? Well, it seems it was a bit special. It's what's called a macaw and was a prize-winner at bird shows. Anyway, the guy that owns it had offered a reward and I'm going to get it!" His wife looked at him and he could see the cogs going round. "Are you now going to tell me that the bike has a reward as well," she asked. "No," he said, with a little grin, "but I expected I'd get the reward for the parrot and I took the bike sort of on approval – if you approve of it it's ours, so what do you say?"

'After some thought, his wife said, "I say you're a cheeky devil and you were pushing your luck – but I like the idea of the bike, so let's take it!" Archie gave her a big hug and the spare crash helmet, in that order, and said, "Hop on, love, we've got an errand to do. We're off to the Red Lion in Charlford and we're going to suggest the words Parrot, Apple tree, and Motorbike for their Tell-A-Tale competition and see if anybody can come up with a decent story!"' Boots paused, then ended with, 'As I hope I've done.'

After a second or two of silence the folk in the room realised he'd finished, decided he'd done a really good job of it and burst into a round of applause with cries of, 'Well done the lads!', 'Come on and give us another one!', 'Reckon you've got a winner there, Jim', and 'How about a bit of music, if you're a band?'

Boots shrugged it off, pleased to have got through to a reasonable finish, and looked round for Slim or Whacker to give him some cover to get out of the room. Slim was nowhere to be seen but Whacker grabbed his arm. 'Well done, mate! Are you goin' to give them another one?' he asked, all excited by the response.

'No, that's enough for me, let's get out into some fresh air and relax a bit – that was tougher than I'd expected.'

So, they went out to the Beer Garden and found a table that was empty apart from a few glasses. Before they could sit down a voice said, 'Here, let me clear that for you, and these are on the house.' With that, a tray with three full glasses was put down, and the girl who'd booked them in that afternoon rapidly collected all the empties.

'Hang on a minute,' said Whacker, 'what are these for? And how come you're still here after office hours?'

'I wouldn't look a gift horse in the mouth, if I were you!' she replied, a bit indignantly. 'After all, they were sort of won by your pal here and his storytelling. And Dad's not often splashed out like this.'

'Ah,' said Whacker, 'so your dad works here as well, does he? And that's why you're late, waiting for a lift home. I get it now.'

At this, the girl burst out laughing, 'You don't get it at all, silly. You see, my dad owns the place, so I live here and help out wherever help is needed – and he really needs help dealing with little detectives like you!!'

'Sorry,' said Whacker, 'I guess I should mind my own business.'

'No problem, but just relax, you're among friends, as long as you ignore some of the loudmouths in the bar, so you might find it's best to use the Residents' Lounge.' And she turned to go.

'Before you go,' said Boots, 'it looks like you've brought a drink for our mate Slim, so do you know where he is?'

'Sorry, I've not seen him since he left after talking to DC Cole – have you tried his room?'

'We'll try that, but who's DC Cole?'

'Local bobby – Detective Constable actually, and based in Salchester, but he lives in the village so we call him our local bobby.'

'Oops, good job you mentioned Slim talking to him – I came in to phone my parents and got sidetracked,' said Whacker. 'Do you think I could use the phone in reception and put it on my bill, cos I've not got enough change for the pay phone?'

'Me too,' joined in Boots.

'OK,' she replied, 'I'll just tell Dad where I am and let you into the office.'

'Sorry to take you away from whatever you're supposed to be doing,' said Whacker, as she led the way and unlocked the office door, mentally kicking himself for not having a better chat-up line.

'That's all right, it's a pleasant change to get away from clearing the tables and the like. And I don't often have somebody different to talk to. I know all the regulars, and our visitors are usually family groups or serious walkers, and they don't really see me as a person – just part of the pub fixtures and fittings!'

Whacker thought they must be blind, as he reckoned the girl was not just good-looking, but really nice. The problem was, he didn't know what to do about it, particularly now that he wasn't at all sure who or what she was referring to when she said 'somebody different'. If she meant 'nice different', she probably meant Boots, but if it was 'odd different', then he was probably the person she meant. He knew that what he really needed was a fail-proof chat-up line, but where or when he'd get one was anybody's guess. So, as always in these situations, he decided it was best to keep quiet.

The moment was gone when she said, 'I'll leave you to make your call while I go and collect your friend to make his.' Whacker didn't know whether to kick himself or feel relieved that he'd not made a fool of himself, and it took him a minute to get his thoughts sorted out before he could ring home and tell them the essence of what had happened that day. He'd just hung up when Boots came in and looked at him a bit oddly. But he said nothing, just made his own call home.

Both sets of parents said they'd love to come along for a day out on Sunday. But before the lads left the office, Boots asked Whacker what had happened with the waitress/receptionist. 'That young lady came out of here with a quiet smile on her face. So what you been and gone and done this time, me old mate?'

'Nothing, honest! I really wanted to at least pay her a compliment, but didn't know what to say. So I guess I must have blushed and she saw right through me. But was she really looking happy when she came out?'

'Course she was. No matter what you said or didn't say, I reckon she likes you, so just be careful and don't spoil things for the rest of us – we don't want her old man kicking us out. Come and have that drink I won for you!!'

So they returned to the Beer Garden and found Slim already well into his drink, having been told about them when he'd turned up at the bar. They brought him up to date on their own activities and discoveries, but Slim was quiet about his own.

'What do we do now, then?' asked Whacker. 'I feel a bit in limbo. It's not like it used to be when we were backpacking – at this time in the evening we'd be cleaning up after supper and getting the tents set up for the night, but there's none of that to do. I thought it would be great not having chores and such, but there's only so much sitting around you can do.'

'Yes, you're right for a change,' agreed Slim. 'So, how about going out for that walk we started when we first got here?' With that he finished his drink, got up and headed for the gate leading to the lane down to the ford. Exchanging puzzled looks, the other two did likewise, and the trio ended the day, gazing into the slow-moving stream in quiet contemplation.

Chapter 7

The sounds and scents of breakfast being served and enjoyed brought the lads down to the dining room and the company of Mr and Mrs Wilkinson with whom they exchanged the usual greetings and enquiries about how they'd slept. Earlier instructions from Slim prevented Whacker from telling them in detail either about his dreams last night or about Boots' snoring.

'That was lovely, Tina,' said Mrs W, as her plate was cleared away. 'Could we have some more coffee, please?' If she noticed Boots and Whacker look at each other and smile at learning Tina's name, Mrs W made no mention of it but smiled to herself. Instead, she turned to them and asked, 'Is it still on for Mr W and me to come with you down to the Manor House? We don't want to be a nuisance, but it would be nice to be introduced to the new owner.'

'Oh yes, that's still the plan,' said Slim, this time without 'the plan' being in capital letters. 'If you can give us a couple of minutes to collect our instruments after breakfast we can meet up in reception – we haven't agreed a time to be there, but there's plenty to do.'

'Are you sure we won't be in the way? We really only wanted to have a look round for old times' sake.'

'You'll be fine, and I'm sure Mr Philips will be pleased to meet you and perhaps get some of the history of the place. For instance, he's moved heaps of stuff out of the house and can't decide what to do with a lot of it – not sure if it might be important or valuable, I suppose.' This was Boots; he seemed to be most in tune with the overall situation, while Whacker couldn't stop wondering about the offered drum kit, and Slim seemed to be worrying about the audition and gig.

Some twenty minutes later, the five of them set off in the early morning sunshine, fairly comfortable in each other's company but lost for what to talk about apart from the weather – 'Whether it'll rain or not!!' chortled Mr W, before his wife could dig him in the ribs. She'd tried to impress on him yet again that not everybody shared his sense of humour, particularly the younger generation!

When the Manor House came into view they all stopped and looked. In the morning sunshine, the sandstone details around the windows and doors really stood out in contrast to the red brick walls. The lads hadn't seen it before from this distance and in this light and it made them realise what a lovely building it was, though perhaps smaller than they first thought. On the other hand, the Wilkinsons thought it looked larger than they remembered it, perhaps because they'd spent more time inside it. But it was quiet, no sign of Mr Philips or any of the girls who had brought life to place yesterday afternoon.

'Did yesterday really happen?' asked Whacker, suddenly wondering if the prospect of the drum kit had all been part of a dream.

'Course it did, they're probably just doing things inside,' said Slim, taking charge again. 'Probably round the back in the stable yard – I bet the girls are sorting out some of the stuff we saw yesterday looking for fancy dress costumes – you know what girls are like when there's a party to get ready for.'

As he was about to set off, Mrs W held them back saying, 'I think it's more polite to try the front door first – we don't actually know that they're in the stable block, do we?'

So that's what they did but, before they could knock on the door, it was opened by a beaming Tony Philips. 'You're all here then, bright and early, and whose parents are you?' (*I don't need to say that he was addressing Mr & Mrs W, do I?*)

'We're not...'

'They're not...'

'One at a time, please, and sorry if I offended...'

Mrs W jumped into the pause. 'Right, we're not with the lads – well we are, as we're all staying at the Red Lion – but we only met them yesterday and they said they'd bring us along and introduce us to the new owner – er – I assume that's you, sir'.

'I see, so what can I do for you, Mrs...?'

'Sorry, sir, we're Mr & Mrs Wilkinson. And the only thing we'd really like you to do for us is to just let us look at the old house. You see, we used to work here, my hubby and I, and now we've finished work we thought we'd like to see some of the old places we've been to or worked in, sort of...' Mrs W tailed off, thinking it was all a bit of an imposition.

But Tony Philips's eyes lit up. 'You used to work here? Wow – just what I need, somebody who knows what should go where. But if you're wanting a job I'm afraid I'm not looking for staff, just some occasional help.'

'We're happy to help with that, sir, if it gives us a bit more of a look at the old place.'

'That's settled, then, just a bit of help over the weekend, not to make you change any plans, is that right? And please don't call me "sir" – just Mr Philips or Tony, OK?'

'Just as you wish, sir.'

At this, Tony looked up to the heavens but decided to carry on, 'Right now I need to have a word with the lads so, if you really mean it about helping out, it would be a great help right now if you could make us a coffee – would that be all right? I'm living in the cottage at the moment, so you'll find the makings in there. I'll be in here with the lads first off, then we'll go out to the stable yard, and I think that would be the best place for our break – if you're really sure you don't mind?'

The smiles and nods from Mr and Mrs W were all he needed, and off they all went.

In the cottage, things hadn't changed much since the Wilkinsons had lived there themselves some fifteen years before, even down to the crockery and cutlery being in the same drawers. So, once they'd found the ingredients, they got on with making up a tray. 'It seems funny, you know,' said Mrs W, 'with the master of the house living in here. He's quite different from the old family, isn't he? We'd best play it a bit steady till we see how the land lies.'

In the Manor House, Tony stood with the lads in the entrance hall, not quite sure how to put things. 'Look, lads, I'm afraid there won't...I'm sorry but er... look, I've spoken to the DJ chap and circumstances mean we can't find a time for you to play this evening. When I booked him to do the party I knew his timing was all a bit tight. He's doing the sound system for a garden party this afternoon and can't be sure when he'll get away, so the whole of our start-up music is pre-programmed ready for me just to switch it on, so he tells me, and can't be adjusted. I'm really sorry lads – I know Anna liked what you did. The best I can offer is for you to play during the barbecue tomorrow afternoon, that is, if you're still in the village and not got anything else planned.'

All three thought that this was probably a roundabout way of not letting them play, but Slim knew they shouldn't give up at the first obstacle, so he checked that the other two were with him then said, 'Yes, we'll do it – but only if we do an audition for you first. And we can do that now if it's convenient.'

So they moved out onto the front lawn, as that was where they would be playing, and unpacked their guitars. Tony expected Whacker to go and get the drum he'd been working on, but Whacker explained that it still needed setting up properly so he'd do what he normally did, which was to hold Slim's solid guitar case a bit like you'd hold a double bass, then beat the rhythm with his hands.

The lads had already decided to do the same numbers they'd played for the girls – 'Autumn Morning' followed by 'Charlbury Moon' – so that if Mr Philips wanted to discuss it with his daughter, at least they'd be talking about the same things.

It should have felt relaxed and fun like it always did when they ran through numbers when they were out backpacking, but this was an actual audition with the chance of a proper gig resting on it, so it felt a bit tense and they weren't too happy at the end. Fortunately, Tony didn't seem to notice and was very surprised and pleased to realise he actually did enjoy their music.

'Right, lads, you're on for tomorrow, if the usual terms apply,' he said, 'i.e. you play for your lunch and keep any money that gets thrown in your hat, OK?'

They all looked absolutely gobsmacked – yes, they'd passed the audition for the gig, but instead of a few quid as a fee, they had to put a hat down and be like buskers!! But when the shock wore off, they realised it wasn't a bad deal for a first outing, particularly as they expected the audience to be friendly – all they needed to do now was to get a hat to catch any coins!!

'Now,' said Tony, keen to get on with his own problems, 'the barbecue will be over there, by the edge of the lawn, so I think you'd be best off stationed in the gazebo next to it. Then you can judge when people have settled down for you to start. Oh, and you know your parents are welcome to join us for that if they're coming down.'

'Oh yes, sorry,' said Whacker, 'forgot to tell you that my mum and dad will be coming, and Dad is really looking forward to seeing the coach. And they're bringing Boots' mum, if that's OK. She says it's just for the outing, but I reckon she really wants to have a look at the tapestries here in the house and perhaps any interesting fabrics in the stuff out in the carriage house. Hope that's OK.'

'Yes, it's fine,' replied Tony, with a smile – he'd found these lads so easy to be with and to talk to, particularly after being on his own so much since he'd come to Charlford. 'As for today, I leave it to you if you want to have another go at cleaning up the drums, or perhaps do a bit of dusting in the carriage ready for your dad to see. But do feel free to go off and do what you planned to do this weekend – I tend to forget that you didn't set out just to give me a hand. If you're staying, you can use any materials you find, though I don't know if we have any suitable tools for work on the drums.'

'What about the other buildings in the carriage yard?' asked Whacker. 'They must have had a car here, so perhaps one of them was a garage and maybe some tools got left behind – if they could forget to take a coach, they wouldn't have fussed over a few spanners!'

Before Tony could reply they were startled by a scraping and squeaking sound at the rear of the hall and turned to see a previously hidden door open to reveal Mr W carrying a picnic basket. 'Sorry to disturb you, sir, but we couldn't decide what drinks would be suitable for the young gentlemen so we made up flasks of soft drinks in addition to the coffee you requested.'

Wow! Mr W was in genuine butler mode, and the lads, particularly Whacker, were really knocked back – they'd never been referred to as 'young gentlemen' before, and it felt good. They all decided that, if this was the treatment rock stars got, they'd better make a good job of tomorrow's gig and hope it was the first step to stardom.

'That's brilliant Mr Wilkinson,' said Tony, 'but we're finished in here so I think we'll take them out to the stable yard. We need to look for some spanners and things. I've got keys to the coach houses, but I don't know how to get into the other building out there.'

'Which building is that, sir? There were only five that were kept locked in my time, the coach houses and the laundry room.'

'Then I guess it must be the laundry room. But why would it be called that? It's a bit far from the house, isn't it?' asked Tony.

'Yes, but in the days when it was used for laundry it kept that "unseemly" side of the servants' work away from the family and, more importantly, away from any guests. Even then, they often had to keep the doors closed when they worked in there so as not to offend people going to and from the stables. Of course, it all changed when electricity arrived and they installed washing machines in the below stairs area of the Manor House itself. The laundry room then became a general workshop and I kept items I needed for car maintenance in there.'

'So, you were a chauffeur, then?'

'And the rest, sir!! My original role at the house was to assist the gardener, then it went on to cleaning the car, and I also began doing odd jobs around the place. Both the gardener and the chauffeur were getting on a bit and when each of them retired I was just expected to take over their roles.'

'Sounds like too much for one man if you'd previously been assisting the other two,' interrupted Tony.

'It might have been, but by this time the household was a lot smaller. The younger members had gone off to follow their own careers, so it all suited me as well as it did the family.'

'So why did you leave? Oops, sorry, none of my business, but it sounds like a reasonable set-up. I assume Mrs W was part of the domestic staff, so you'd have a roof over your heads and not far to go to work every day.'

'No. I don't mind us telling you about it – it's the main reason why we're here, but I'd like Mrs W to join us, if you don't mind, sir. The next bit's mainly hers.'

'That's fine by me,' replied Tony, 'but can you get us into this laundry building before you go to get her? Then young Whacker here can help me sort out any tools that might be of use.'

When they got to the door of the mystery building, Mr W sorted through the bunch of keys Tony had been given and found the two they needed – one for the door itself and one for the padlock. Mr W explained that two locks had been needed because the remoteness of the house had made it, and its outbuildings, a target for thieves. 'In those days, sir, there were no intruder alarms or security lights, of course.'

'But what about whoever lived in the cottage or slept above the stables?' asked Tony. 'Wouldn't their presence put off any thieves?'

'Not really likely, sir, and security wasn't a duty that many of them would be willing to undertake on top of their more-or-less full-time duties in the house. No, the cottage and the over-stable rooms were a bit of a sanctuary – at least it seems that they were in the old days. Much more reasonable in our time here, but we still needed a place of our own when off duty.' Leaving the others to look inside the building, Mr W went off to find his wife.

Inside the laundry room there were tools, cans of oil, and such stuff arranged neatly on shelves along the back wall as well as on the top of a square brick-built thing in the back corner of the room. Closer inspection of this construction revealed what looked like a door to a fireplace in one of its sides. It had the lads puzzled, but Tony explained that it was what was called a copper. Inside the brickwork would be a huge copper tub that could be filled with water and then heated by a fire under it, all for washing the bed linen and clothes from the house.

They had just opened the fireplace door when Mrs W arrived and uttered a loud gasp, 'Oh, please be careful if you look in there,' she almost wailed, clasping her hands to her mouth as if to stifle a sob.

Her husband, hot on her heels, put a calming hand on her shoulder and asked Tony, 'Do you mind if I have a look in there first, please, sir? You see, we hid some papers inside the fireplace some years ago and it would mean so much to my wife if we found they were still there.'

Tony, looking rather shocked, asked, 'This isn't something you stole from the house, is it? Or anything else of a criminal nature? Cause if it is, the lads here mustn't be involved, and I need to be sure there'll be no comeback on me.'

'Oh no, sir, nothing like that, I assure you,' said Mrs W, now slightly recovered. 'All we hope to find in there are some little notes that Mr W gave me and I wanted them to be kept secret. You see, we weren't married at the time – well, I was – but my then husband, who was the butler, had become a bit of a brute, and Mr W used to leave me little funny notes to try to cheer me up, and I kept them. As I think you've probably already guessed, we eventually fell in love and the notes became love letters. We were going to come clean about it to the master and mistress, but my husband found one of the notes before I could get to it, and raised merry hell. So, I asked Mr W to hide the rest for me and this was the best place he could think of that no-one else from the house normally came to. Unfortunately, when my husband told the master what he'd found, the master reacted very quickly, and we were both dismissed instantly. We were given only enough time to pack our belongings, so we had no chance to collect the papers. This is the first time we've been able to get back here and I suppose we really must assume that they've been found or burnt before now.'

'Well,' said Tony, 'what a turn up, and what a romantic tale! Come on Mr W, get the fire door open and let's see if your letters and your secret have been kept safe. And you, lads, keep all this to yourselves – no gossip up in the village, OK?'

'Yeah!'

'Of course.'

'No probs, but the story might find its way into a song some time,' said Boots with a smile. 'But anonymously, of course!'

It would have been too much to expect the letters to be there still, and of course they weren't. So, both a wonderful story and Mrs W's hopes came to an abrupt end. She had everyone's sympathy but, fortunately, everyone had other things to do so she didn't have to spend too long responding and trying to look cheerful before she could return to the peace and quiet of the main house with her husband.

Chapter 8

After their morning drinks and the mild excitement of Mrs W's quest, the lads started talking about a set list for the following day, but their hearts weren't in it. Then at midday Mrs W called them to join them along with Philips's and Anna's friends for a light lunch of sandwiches, crisps and a cold drink out at the front of the main house. They found various garden chairs and enjoyed a relaxed meal, chatting about everything and nothing in particular. As soon as politely possible, Anna excused herself and her friends to go and decide what to wear for the evening; after that the group soon broke up.

Whacker wanted to get on with cleaning up a couple of drums, having found a drum key taped inside the frame of the bass drum. (*A drum key is a simple tool designed to help dismantle and/or tune up a drum.*)

Boots felt at a bit of a loose end, so followed the Wilkinsons into the main house to see if they could tell him anything about its history or the paintings or tapestries.

Slim therefore found it easy to slip away up to the village saying he'd got something to do – and did he have something to do!! He was intent on solving, or at least helping to solve, the puzzle of all the burglaries that DC Cole had told him about the night before in the inn.

First stop was the Lounge Bar of the Red Lion to look through the latest editions of the local papers but, it being at least two weeks since the last burglary, the only mention was that the police were continuing with their enquiries. However, it did give the name of the villages where the crimes had been committed, so Slim set off to walk to the nearest one, it being only a couple of miles away. What he really needed first was the address of the house that had been burgled and he had an idea on how to go about getting it.

As he approached the village it looked like he was in luck for there, kicking a ball about on a bit of rough ground, was a group of three or four young boys. He slowed down so that he was passing them when the ball bounced his way. He kicked it back to them and asked if the police were still at the burgled house, as he had a message for them. The boys told him, somewhat cheekily, that if he knew anything about it, he'd see there was no-one there as it was the first house in the village, right in front of them!

While deciding how to respond to that, Slim looked up and saw a man, leading a dog, step out of the house and head towards his garden gate. He quickly nipped forward to intercept the man, saying, 'Sorry to interrupt your walk, sir, but I understand yours is one of the houses that was burgled recently.'

'And who are you, then? The Press again, or trying to sell me some security gimmick? Clear off! I've had a belly full!'

Not the response that Slim had expected but he managed to bring out the story he'd prepared.

'Oh no, nothing like that. You see, I live at home with my mum and these burglaries have got her quite worried, particularly as I'm likely to move out when I start my training, and I wondered if the police had given you any useful tips you could pass on about home security. I mean, I would have thought your dog was a good deterrent, so perhaps we should get one.'

'No they didn't,' the man replied, still quite aggressively. 'And the dog was no use then, was he? We were away in the caravan, dog and all! So, if you want any advice, go and ask the police yourself, and stop bothering me!'

With that, he turned away and walked off, pulling his dog along. Slim stood there not sure what to do next except set off back to Charlford, the taunts from the kids ringing in his reddening ears; 'You from the police? Don't think so!' 'Not from round here, so clear off!'

But all was not lost, it was only the first foray. This uplift of mood was triggered by the arrival of a local bus on its way towards Salchester. Slim caught it just to get to the next village and repeat his procedure on the next burglary victim.

This time he had more luck in that he got directions to the house from a woman with a pushchair. He told her his story about his mum being worried about home security and gained her sympathy and support. In fact, she insisted on taking him to the house in question and introducing him to the owner's wife. Again, the family had been on holiday, but in this case their dog had been in boarding kennels. The woman happily gave him the kennels' address in case he and his mum did get a dog, and off he went, happier than he expected to be, and ready to repeat the process at as many of the burgled houses as he could find.

Slim only managed to find two more 'victim' houses when he realised he ought to get back to Charlford before the buses stopped for the evening. He also needed to have a cover story in case Boots and Whacker got too interested in what he'd been doing. But that shouldn't be a problem, he decided, as they both seemed absorbed in the Manor House and all that went with it. He'd tell them he'd been walking, enjoying the fresh air, seeking inspiration for more songs, and they couldn't dispute that!

In the event, Slim didn't need a cover story at all because the lads, as he'd guessed, had been engrossed in things at the Manor House and hadn't really missed him, each assuming that he was with the other one.

Whacker had cleaned up a couple of the drums very nicely and found a pair of brushes but no sticks, so his backing rhythm would be nice and soft rather than strident. They'd all feared that the use of a proper drum might sound too harsh, particularly as they were all acoustic. Once or twice Whacker had used a tambourine borrowed from school, but it had long ago lost its bells, and that had been OK for sound level, but not for the impression they wanted to give!

Boots, on the other hand, (*sorry, no mixed pun intended, but you can't say 'on the other foot', can you?*) he'd spent the afternoon in and around the house; essentially, that had been wherever Anna had happened to be! And she wasn't trying to avoid him!

Slim couldn't decide whether to be a bit put out that he'd not really been missed, or be pleased that he'd not had to answer awkward questions. On balance, it felt better to keep quiet about his activities until he had some positive results to report.

As teatime approached, Mr and Mrs W and the lads were tidying up ready to return to the village when Tony called them all together.

'I just want to thank you all for all your help today. I'd not realised how much would need to be done, particularly all the small things that are easily forgotten and seem to take more time than you'd imagine. Honestly, I couldn't have managed without you and the party would have been off to a late start. As you know, this evening is all fixed up, otherwise I'd invite you to join us. So, I hope you don't mind but, to show my appreciation, I've phoned the Red Lion and asked them to bill me with whatever food and drink you have this evening. And I do hope you'll be able to come and join us and enjoy the barbecue tomorrow – I promise not to ask you to help out!!'

They chorused their thanks, mixed with comments that they'd really enjoyed the day – payment not necessary – have a great evening, sir, etc. Then off on the walk to the village and a real rest.

Chapter 9

Back at the Red Lion, after a speedy wash and brush-up, all five of them arrived more or less together at the dining room, and found Tina just inside the door checking over the list of bookings for the evening.

'I hope you are here as a group,' she said. 'All we have clear at the moment is the six-seater in the corner, and that's only available because of a cancellation. It will be at least half an hour before enough of the smaller tables clear for you to sit in your two groups.'

It took only a quick look at each other to agree they'd be OK in one group. 'As long as you don't start telling silly jokes!' Mrs W quietly warned her husband who replied, with a chuckle, 'As if I would!'

Once they were seated Mrs W took on the role of mum and started to ask the boys what they'd been doing all day until she stopped with a giggle, realising they'd more or less shared the day's activities. 'But we haven't seen much of you, Slim – anything special you want to share with us?' she asked.

'No, not really. But if things go as well tomorrow, I might have something special to report tomorrow evening.' Then he clammed up and wouldn't say another word on the subject despite all the pressure from Boots and Whacker, like, 'Is it a girl, Slim?' 'It's not Tina, is it?' 'I bet you're doing something to try and impress that police bloke you were chatting to yesterday, right?' This final point almost forced a response.

But it all stopped when Tina appeared at the table to take their orders. 'I guess Mr Philips told you that this meal is on him?' she asked, and they all nodded. 'I'm sure the lads won't take advantage of his generosity, will they Mr Wilkinson?' she asked. Realising she was putting the responsibility for their actions on him, Mr W smiled and said, 'Don't worry, my dear, they're good lads and I'm sure they don't need me or the wife to keep an eye on them. Mind you, the way they've worked today they'll need proper man-size portions, no kiddies' menus for them, love.' And chuckled and got a glare from his wife.

All three lads squirmed a bit at being treated as if they needed to be reminded to behave properly, but they nodded their agreement, and Tina managed to organise their responses into an understandable set of orders.

Once Tina had moved away, Mrs W led the conversation away from Slim's activities by asking, 'Who's mums and dads are coming along tomorrow, then? I bet they're looking forward to hearing you perform.'

'I believe my mum's getting a lift with Whacker's mum and dad,' said Boots, 'but I've not said anything to them about the gig. Have you, Whacker, to yours?'

'No, never thought about it. I want my dad here mainly to look at the drum kit for me, then Tony and me both want him to look at the coach or carriage, whatever you're supposed to call it.'

'What carriage is that?' asked Mrs W, leaning towards Whacker very eagerly.

'One we found yesterday in the coach house – if it's in a coach house I guess it's got to be a coach, hasn't it? Anyway, nobody knew it was there. According to Tony it wasn't listed as part of what he bought – you know, the house and everything – so he's not even sure if it's his legally or not. But my dad knows a bit about coaches so Tony's asked for him to come and look at it and see if he can tell him anything about it. It might be rare and valuable, and worth selling, but then again perhaps it just got forgotten by the previous owners who'll turn up one day to collect it. Nobody knows anything about it. All very interesting, my dear Watson!!' he finished, in what he thought was a good Sherlock Holmes impression.

'You're wrong there, young master Whacker,' replied Mrs W, 'my hubby and I know a fair bit about it, and so we should because it's almost the reason we're together, isn't it, Harry?'

'Too true, my love, and when you think about it, it's no wonder the master left it behind – less fuss than raking over that particular episode in the family story AND having to explain it to the younger generations – that would have caused a right chuckle.' In case they'd not understood him, Mr W illustrated what he meant with a long low belly-rumbling chuckle. This caused Mrs W to demonstrate her chuckle-control technique comprising a swift dig in his ribs accompanied by a strong sideways glare.

'What's the story then?' asked Whacker, starting to look a bit upset. 'I hope my dad's not coming down for nothing!'

'Don't forget the drums, mate,' interjected Boots, 'and he might find some interesting joints or carvings or whatever he wants to find. Don't forget there's all that furniture as well as the coach.'

'Yes, lad, don't get upset,' joined in Mr W, 'but I reckon he'll be interested in the story of how the coach came to be locked away and forgotten, so get on with it, Mary.'

But before she could start, their drinks were served and Mrs W needed to wet her whistle, then she began the story by pointing out that it all started some twenty-odd years before.

'By that time the family had grown up, and the young ones had drifted away, so there was only the master and mistress living there more or less full time, and it had become a very odd staff situation. There was a butler, old Mr Hawkins, though there was rarely a need for a butler, and my then-husband, Phil Jenkins, was footman, chauffeur, and part-time valet to the master. People just had to adapt to different roles when visitors or family were there.'

Another pause when their starters were served and Mrs W was nudged by her husband to not let her soup go cold; this gave her a moment to collect her thoughts and memories.

'One of the things that generally didn't affect the household staff, though, was any help that was needed getting the carriage ready for use – and putting it away afterwards. When the family was younger and there were horses in the stables, for riding and for carriage work, there was always a stable lad or groom to harness the horses, get the carriage ready for the master to drive, and then clean up and put it all away when he came back.'

'Sorry,' interrupted Boots, 'did you say the master drove the carriage? I always thought these people had proper coachmen, like the Queen has.'

'Yes, but driving the carriage, or coach, was one of the master's hobbies, if you like. He didn't use it to go on journeys, as such, just to get out and about around the area – call on friends, and so on. Mind you, the number of friends prepared to have a coach and horses parked outside their home for a couple of hours was getting few and far between.'

'So, what had this got to do with the butler and you two getting together?' asked Whacker, hoping he'd remember all this to tell his dad next day.

'Well, when there were only the carriage horses left in the stables and no live-in stable staff, a chap used to come in from the village every day to look after them, get them fed, watered and so on, and harnessed-up when needed. But if the master got back home early from a drive and the chap hadn't arrived yet to help, he'd shout for Mr Hawkins, the butler. Unfortunately, old Hawkins and the master didn't really get along very well and, on top of that, Mr Hawkins didn't like horses – in fact I did hear say that he was afraid of them. So, he always took his time getting out there in the hope that somebody else, like my hubby here, would beat him to it.'

Another pause while their main courses were served and started on, then Mr W took over. 'I don't think you said, love, that I was there as gardener, odd-job man and so on. Anyway, on one occasion when I was working outside, I heard the master call and went to help. We easily got the horses unhitched and taken to the stable, but the real problem had been in reversing the coach to get it into the coach house – the horses didn't like it, and the carriage was too heavy for one person to push. The master had obviously been thinking about this problem and asked me if I could fix a couple of ringbolts in the coach house – one in the middle of the floor and one a couple of feet up in the middle of the back wall. And would I also get a long piece of rope, thin enough to pass through the rings.'

A pause while Mr W attacked his steak again, then – 'So in the next couple of days I got the job done, wondering what the heck it was all for! If one of the ringbolts had been for inside the roof, I'd have thought he was going to hang either himself or old Hawkins!!' The Wilkinson rumble chuckle took over and Mrs W made him stop talking, take a breath, have a sip of water, and eat more of his meal.

'So, what was it all for?' asked Whacker. 'And I hope it's not too complicated for me to explain to my dad.'

'No, we're nearly there, lad, and you'll be able to set it up to show your dad tomorrow. What he did was pass the rope through both ringbolts, and the end that came up through the ring in the wall was tied to the coach somewhere below the driver's bench seat, I seem to remember. The rope end that came forward through the ringbolt in the floor was attached to the horses' harness. Here, let me try and draw it for you.'

So saying, Mr W took the pencil from the spine of his pocket diary, tore an empty page from it and drew a simple diagram to show the path the rope took.

'Don't ask me to draw the horses, anybody, but they'd be here at the front end. The master then unhitched them from the coach so they were only attached to the end of the rope – see? He then led the horses forward; this pulled the rope through the ring in the floor, then through the one in the back wall and up to the carriage, pulling it back into the coach house. There.'

'That's ingenious!' exclaimed Slim, deciding it was time he showed a little interest in the topic. 'He must have been a bit of an engineer.'

This brought general murmurings of agreement, allowing Mr W to look pleased with himself and take another mouthful of his food.

'Hang on a minute though,' said Whacker, 'you still haven't said how the coach – or carriage – brought you two together. Were you holding the horse or something, or have I missed a bit?'

'No, we haven't got to that part yet,' laughed Mrs W, 'but shall we just finish eating first? Then, if you can sit while your dinner settles, we can tell you the rest.'

'Is it going to take long?' asked Slim. 'Cos we ought to be having a final run-through for tomorrow. I'm not saying it's not interesting, of course,' he added hurriedly, though he was far less interested than the other two seemed to be.

'Ease up a bit, Slim,' said Whacker, 'we've got all tomorrow morning to have a final run-through. Let's just relax for once, OK?' Whacker was just realising how much effort he'd put into cleaning the drums and, after all, they'd not come to Charlford to work!

Without any further chat on the subject they finished their meals with comments about how good the food and service were, how nice not have to wash the pots, etc. They were each wondering who should make the next move when Tina, arriving and asking if they'd like to have coffee in the Residents' Lounge, made the decision for them. Most customers on a Saturday evening were, understandably, in either the bar or the dining room so they had the Lounge to themselves. Once settled with their coffees – tea for Slim – Mr W took up the tale about the Manor House and the carriage – or coach.

'The master tried out his device a couple of times while the groom chap was there and was thrilled to bits with it. I reckon this was mainly because he'd designed it and partly because he was less dependent on the groom being there when he came back from a drive. He tried out different ways of doing it and finally decided he should attach the rope to the coach before he tied it to the horses.'

'Why's that, then?' asked Whacker, wanting to be sure he got it right when he told his dad.

'The first time he tried it, he attached it to the horses' harness first and something he did must have spooked one of them. They pulled forward and were almost out of the yard before the groom could stop them – and, of course, with the other end of the rope not connected to the coach, they'd pulled it all the way out, so it needed to be re-threaded through the bolts. Quite a palaver!' And another chuckle at the memory.

While Mr W paused for a drink of his coffee his wife sort of apologised to the lads. 'Sorry for all that detail but you really do need to get the picture in your mind's eye, to help you imagine what could go wrong,' and she finished with a chuckle that could have been caused by a bit of embarrassment or by a recollection of the events about to be described.

'Things went wrong,' continued Mr W, 'the day when the master brought back some cushions that a friend had sent for the mistress to look at. He'd carried them on the luggage rack on top of the coach and later explained to his wife, "One doesn't convey parcels inside one's carriage – that would make it no better than a tradesman's delivery van!"' Mr W had delivered this in what he believed sounded like a hoity-toity voice and it raised a laugh all round.

'Normally,' he went on, 'if the groom wasn't there, he'd connect up the rope system, lead the horses forward himself, untie the rope from their harness when the coach was back where he wanted it, then lead the horses to the stable for the groom to deal with them when he arrived. This time, though, it seems that he'd set it all up before he remembered the parcel of cushions on top of the coach. Trusting the horses to stand still, he climbed up onto the driving seat and leaned back to pick up the parcel of cushions – with me so far? Well, that was when disaster struck – in the form of old Hawkins.'

Mrs W took up the tale – 'Mr Hawkins had taken a phone call for the master – up in the Manor House, of course – but couldn't find anyone to go and look for him, so off he went himself. He'd felt the call was important, even urgent, and hurried as fast as his old legs allowed, shouting for the master.'

'I was just about to walk into the yard,' intervened Mr W, 'when I saw and heard old Hawkins, and decided to stay out of it. Hawkins' shouting for the master unnerved the horses and they started forward, pulling on the rope. Naturally the carriage rolled backwards into the coach house as it was intended to do, but this time the master was kneeling on the driver's bench looking back over his shoulder to see what was happening. So he didn't see the top of the doorway before it hit his shoulders and knocked him over. Fortunately, it wasn't far for him to fall into the footwell of the driver's seat – it could have been serious if he'd fallen to the ground from that height.'

'He pulled himself up to his knees and yelled at Hawkins to move the horses back but, of course, Hawkins hated the horses and, in his agitated state, was flapping his arms around like a demented flamingo – not that I've ever seen one – and that made the horses more jittery. At this point, the groom from the village turned up, worked out what was happening and got it all sorted. Unfortunately for the master, his trouser belt or braces had got caught up in something at the driver's bench so, when he finally jumped the last couple of feet to the ground, there was an almighty ripping sound and his trousers were torn off and he was running around in his underwear and knobbly knees!' Another Wilkinson rumble chuckle issued forth and he had to stop to wipe the tears from his eyes in recollection of the scene.

'By this time,' said Mrs W, taking over, 'the racket could be heard far and wide – the master shouting at Hawkins and calling him, amongst other things – a blithering old fool – and telling him he was fired. At the same time Hawkins shouting that he wouldn't work in such a madhouse a minute longer and he resigned and demanded a reference for all the years he'd put up with "things" – though he didn't say what the "things" might be.'

Even the lads were chuckling at this point, picturing scenes like you often get in cartoons or Laurel and Hardy films. Boots was the first to get back to the topic and ask where Mr and Mrs W getting together came into the story.

'I suppose you could say it all really started from that point,' said Mrs W. 'Who knows if the master really meant what he'd said to Mr Hawkins, but the old chap went straight to his room and began packing ready to leave next morning. The master found himself without a butler, and that would never do. So, to fill the gap, my then-husband, Phil, was made butler.'

'And I took her old man's place as chauffeur – on top of carrying on as gardener-cum-handyman,' added Mr W.

'This was all OK for a while,' continued Mrs W, 'but the problem was that Phil – my husband – hadn't been trained as a butler, and he'd never expected to become one, so he hadn't really watched and learned what Mr Hawkins had actually done and been expected to do. Fortunately – or as time passed I began to wonder if it was perhaps unfortunately – I'd taken notice of the butler's duties and was able to give Phil pointers on occasion. But he was a proud man and took my tips as being criticisms of his failings. So, it wasn't long before he began snapping at me, and then it got worse – no need to go into detail – but people started to notice and that's when my hubby here, bless him, showed his support for me.'

'I couldn't stand by and see her being bullied like that,' interrupted Mr W, 'so I'd have a friendly word if no-one was around, or leave her little notes – nothing untoward – just expressing support and encouragement. I didn't realise that these became precious to her but, when she told me, I helped her hide them, as you know from this morning.'

Mrs W took over the tale again. 'Anyway, the point came when Phil's attitude and behaviour just drove me away from him. He'd suspected for some time that my hubby here had supported me, then he found one of the little notes that confirmed his suspicions and he said straight away that he wanted a divorce. He told the master and mistress – they were quite Victorian in outlook and accepted Phil's suspicions and took his side. So they dismissed both me and my hubby here! We had no option but to leave the house and find jobs somewhere else, preferably together, which we did, and got married – after the divorce of course – and now we're more or less retired together.'

Although he'd been quite interested in their story, Slim had had enough of the Wilkinsons' company and was ready to move off, but didn't know how to do it. Fortunately, Mrs W was well aware that their tale had only limited interest for youngsters, so quickly put in, 'Now you young men have surely got better things to do on a Saturday night than sit and listen to our old stories! Off with you and find some young ladies to chat to!!' So they did – at least they went off, though not necessarily looking for young ladies to chat to.

Outside, where the fish and chip van had been doing such good business the evening before, all was fairly quiet so they headed once more for the footbridge over the Charl, leaned against the guard rail and watched the waters flowing quietly on their way to the sea.

'This is how it should be – how it was meant to be this weekend, you know,' began Slim. 'It all went off course right from the off, and we've not had a minute to ourselves to chat, to write, to rehearse. OK, we've met some nice people, heard some interesting stories, and we've not had to lug our backpacks around and worry about food and that, but it's just not the same!'

'You're right, Slim, me old pal,' agreed Boots, 'but look at all the good bits.'

'Yeah,' interrupted Whacker, 'the band's going to have a decent drum kit! And we get to do a proper gig – not just mates and family.'

'Oh, come on, you two! You both must realise this is just so different from what we've done on backpacking weekends and what we hoped it would be like. I don't know – it feels like we're all going our own ways and it doesn't seem right.'

Boots looked at Whacker in amazement. 'Hang on a bit, Slim, you're the one that disappeared for half the day today and won't say where you went or why – and you're not answering questions about it. Why does all the change suddenly seem to be OUR fault?'

Slim suddenly looked tired. 'Sorry, guys. You're right. I could be on to something really big for me and I suppose I'm stuck between excited as hell and worried sick at the same time. No, no more explanations,' as they both started to speak, 'let's sleep on it and I promise I'll be able to tell you all about it tomorrow – OK? Now let's turn in – big day for us all in the morning.'

And that was the last they spoke before reaching the Red Lion where Slim went straight upstairs to his room. Boots and Whacker headed for the bar to see what was happening but were waylaid by Tina. 'Sorry, lads, the bars are all closed now but if you wanted a coffee or something we could bring it for you in the Residents' Lounge.'

'Thanks all the same,' said Boots, 'but I think I'll turn in – give me half an hour to use the bathroom, Whacker?'

'OK, but don't use all the hot water – gosh that sounds just like my mum!' and Tina joined him in a rueful chuckle. Then he recovered himself and said, 'Now, Miss, may I escort you home and protect you from the ghosties?'

This was totally unplanned and Whacker felt absolutely stupid and started to apologise when Tina interrupted – 'Now then, you know I live on the premises with my dad, but that's a lovely gesture that you don't usually see round here, so Yes, you may walk me home – a quick turn around the village green would do me the world of good. Come on, then, don't stand there looking surprised, you've looked like you wanted to chat me up ever since you arrived, so let's go.' With that she walked out of the front door and an amazed Whacker had to hurry to catch up.

A quick walk around the village green was all it turned out to be, no holding hands, and certainly no kissing, but Whacker was on top of the world and, when they got back to the inn, said a gentle 'Goodnight' then almost floated up to his room, to sleep soundly and dream happily.

CHAPTER 10

Sunday morning started much as it had the day before, but a wee bit later and with The Acolytes feeling the start of the tension that precedes a major gig. On top of this, Whacker experienced an almost electric shock when he accidentally on purpose touched Tina's hand as she brought the toast to their table; he couldn't help both smiling and blushing, though only Tina (and Mrs W) noticed.

The lads hadn't expected to be involved in anything at anyone's home, so only had the clothes they'd travelled in plus spares for meals in the Red Lion. They'd worried about this and mentioned it to the Wilkinsons who'd assured them that their breakfast gear would be fine, 'As long as you don't drip egg all over it,' chuckled Mr W before a dig in the ribs from his wife reminded him to behave.

Before setting off, Whacker checked that his dad would be redirected to the Manor House if he turned up at the inn, Slim checked that he'd got all the music and lists he'd need, while Boots checked that the weather was forecast to be good again – all symptoms of pre-performance nerves. Mr and Mrs W said they'd pop into the church first, but to let Mr Philips know they wouldn't be long and would be there to help, as promised.

On arriving at the Manor, the lads went straight to the stable block that they all subconsciously regarded as their base. Slim and Boots were over the moon when they saw what Whacker had achieved with the drum kit. While he'd only had time to do a full clean and tune on the one snare drum, all the others were at least dusted and set up on their stands so they looked like a proper full set-up – very promising for a future life for the band if you ignored the fact that they'd still not done a proper gig!

Acoustics in the stable were far from good, but good enough for a run-through. This would mainly aim at checking they were all happy with the list for the set (their own 'Autumn Morning', 'Trees For Friends' and 'Rules For

Breaking Up', interspersed with Mystic Wizards' 'Charlbury Moon' and 'The Vulture Song'). As they finished they realised they had an audience of Anna and Bel, followed by Mr W offering them morning coffee up at the house.

'You know,' said Bel, 'I rather like that "Autumn Morning" piece, but I can't decide if it's supposed to be happy or sad.'

'Bit of both,' replied Slim. 'Both the season and the time of day can be either, if you think about it. Though, as for autumn, I usually feel it's a bit sad – the end of summer and start of last part of the year…'

'And don't forget the going-back-to-school feeling after summer holidays,' interjected Whacker.

'And, of course, folk like Whacker mainly see the "having-to-get-out-of-bed" downside of mornings instead of them being the start of a new day, eh, Whacker?' but Boots smiled to remove any censure from the remark.

This discussion looked like it could get too serious for Anna's taste, particularly as it was still her birthday weekend, so she shut it out, leaving it to Bel to carry on chatting to the lads while they packed up for the morning.

Anna had been having mixed feelings about the band right from the start – while it could be cool to have a live band just for her party, if they turned out not to be very good, or too intense, she'd carry the stigma FOR EVER, she thought. Now was the time to decide, and she was stumped. She really, really, liked Boots and she sort of liked the Charlbury and Vulture songs, but wasn't sure about the whole package if that was what she'd just heard. She decided the safest thing was to have a word with her dad and see if he could let them down gently – she really, really, couldn't run the risk of the whole weekend being spoiled and everyone's lasting memory being of three lads singing mournful songs. Yes, Dad would do it, Dad was good at that sort of thing – it's what dads do.

So she nipped up to the house, found her dad on his own, and quickly told him her feelings and misgivings about the lads playing that afternoon. She was a decent girl and didn't lay it on at all, but Tony could see her point and that she was quite upset about what she had done in building up the lads' expectations. After a couple of minutes' thought, he decided what to do and sent Anna back to chat to the lads as if their gig was still on – that way she'd not be blamed for the change of mind. Then, after a few minutes to marshal his thoughts, Tony went down to the stables and interrupted their chat.

'Look, Anna, lads, I don't really know how to say this, but I've had a change of mind about this afternoon's gig.'

Puzzled looks all round led to drooping shoulders, and was that a hint of a tear in Whacker's eye?

'The thing is, lads, a lot of the people who'll be here are family who don't see each other very often and they just want to chat – catch up on family news and so on – right, Anna?' Her downcast head nodded. 'And music in the background would be a distraction or, for some of them, it could drown out the conversation. I know, lads, you're not using amplifiers but some of the older ones are a bit hard of hearing.'

Boots and Slim both started to say something but Tony continued, 'And looking at it from your point of view, I think you'll agree that this might not be the best sort of audience for one of your first gigs, would it? You really want to be playing to a group that all want to listen, don't you? I know you're disappointed and I'm really sorry too for Anna, but I think it's for the best.'

There was a long silence as the lads took in and thought about what he'd said, then they looked at each other, shrugged and nodded in acceptance and left it to Slim to speak for them, as he usually did. 'I guess you're right, Mr Philips, and when we get over the disappointment I think it will help us plan our next move better.'

Seeing Whacker getting ready to say something, Tony anticipated his concern – 'And this doesn't change what I said about the drum kit, in fact I probably feel you deserve it in compensation, so I hope your dad says it's OK and you've got room to have it at home. Of course, I'm looking forward to asking him about the coach, and to meeting all your parents, so I hope you can all still stay and enjoy the barbecue.'

'Actually, Mr Philips, my mum isn't coming,' said Slim, 'she's away for the weekend – so would you mind if I slope off early – there's something I need to do in the next village – Horton?' When the other two looked at him, open-mouthed, Slim went on, 'It's just some information I'm after for a friend. I'll tell you all about it later when it's sorted.'

'That's OK by me, Slim, but do go up to the house and ask Mrs Wilkinson to find you something to eat, won't you? We don't want you passing out in the wilds of the county and have people pointing a finger at me as a rotten host,' and smiled.

With that, Tony turned to head to the house himself and asked Anna to go with him 'to look at one or two of the seating arrangements'.

Out of earshot of the lads she took her dad's arm and gave it a squeeze. 'Thanks so much, Dad, you lied beautifully so I guess I'll have to watch everything you tell me in future!!'

'No, my girl, I'll have to watch that you don't make plans that I have to dig you out of. It won't always be as easy as it was today because what I said about this not being the right first gig for them was true – though what got me thinking like that I'll never know. But they're a genuine bunch of lads. I'm glad you found them and brought them here – they've certainly added something to the weekend.'

Back at the stables Slim could not be persuaded to say what his plans were, but he did promise to be back at the house before the barbecue broke up or, at the very latest, at the Red Lion before the bars closed. He was going to call in at the inn on his way out, so he offered to take Boots' guitar there along with his own, then off he went to the house where Mrs W did indeed find him some sandwiches for a quick lunch.

While Slim was leaving, Mr W was out in the front of the house and met Whacker's dad, his mum and Boots' mum.

He took them into the house and introduced them to Tony who wanted to hustle them down to look at the coach. Mr W prevailed and provided coffees and tea while they relaxed at one of the tables already prepared for the barbecue. He then went to fetch the lads to join their parents, leaving Tony again grateful for the presence of the Wilkinsons.

'Nice place you've got here, Mr Philips,' Whacker's dad opened with.

'Thanks, but please call me Tony, and definitely not "my lord" as your lad wondered about when he first met me!! One of Anna's friends loves to refer to me as the lord of the manor, which of course I'm not, but he took it seriously – I soon put him at ease. They're a nice set of lads and I'm really pleased they've been here – only too sorry that they won't get to play for a suitable audience.'

'Well that's good to know – that they've behaved themselves, I mean,' replied Boots' mum. 'We'd been wondering a bit about the situation as we came along.'

Tony quickly brought them up to speed on what had been happening and, mainly, why he wanted Whacker's dad's opinion on the coach they'd discovered. And that got him to the point where he asked him to come and have a look at it.

'As for the ladies,' he paused, 'while I'm very happy for you to be here, I can't imagine what you'll find of interest to do. So please feel free to wander around or come with us or – I know, let's introduce you to Mrs Wilkinson, she knows more about the house and so on than I do.' So, they were all introduced to Mrs W, then Tony took Whacker's dad – now identified as being Ted Bailey – to look at the coach.

Meanwhile, up at the Red Lion, Slim's arrival alone, but with the two guitar cases, prompted questions from Jim and Tina about the other two lads. He explained what had happened, making it sound like it had been their own decision not to play, rather than the strong suggestion it had really been.

When he asked for directions to get to Skelford, Tina couldn't help but ask what he was looking for there – 'It's only a few houses, you know, no shop or pub, and the church doesn't hold a service every week.'

'What about the kennels?' he asked, rather puzzled.

'Oh, I suppose you mean Skelford Boarding Kennels and Cattery? Well, if you want them, they're not there anymore. They moved a couple of years ago – they're along the Salchester road just before you get to the town.'

'Blow! Looks like I'm not going to get there and back today except by walking – and I'm not sure it's important enough to spend all that time doing that. Why on earth didn't I go there first yesterday?' Although this was Slim berating himself, he said it loud enough for Jim to hear and respond.

'Hang on a minute young man, all's not necessarily lost.' Then he called out to a man sitting in the bar reading the paper, 'Roger, you on choir duty today?'

Without looking up, the man replied with a single, 'Yup.'

'Can you give our friend here a lift to the kennels in town?'

'Yup.'

'Off at the usual time?'

'Yup.'

'There you are then,' to Slim, 'you've got five minutes to take your stuff up to your room and be back down here, ready to go. As they say round here, time and Roger waits for no man, particularly when his Sunday's tied up with getting his wife to and from Cathedral choir duty, like today.'

Not needing any further telling, Slim was off up the stairs and back in a flash. 'Really kind of you to fix it, Mr Parker, it'll be no problem getting back, I'm sure, even if I have to walk it. Oh, and what do I call him – Roger, I mean?'

'Don't worry about that, lad. It's Mr West but, as you see, he doesn't get very chatty but he's a good man. And if you're no more than half an hour at the kennels, I reckon he'd give you a lift back if you're there at the side of the road.'

Suddenly, Slim's spirits were lifted, the Gods must be smiling on him, and even Mr West looked like he was going to be chatty as they walked out to his car. 'You booking yourself into the kennels while your folk go on holiday, then?' and he chuckled and never said another word all the way until he dropped Slim off right outside the kennels.

Chapter 11

At Charlford Manor the barbecue was going as well as Tony Philips had hoped. The food was good and being well appreciated. The distant relatives were all chatting happily with no sign of any backbiting and, most importantly, all the different age groups were mixing well.

Taking the opportunity of a lull in a conversation with Anna's great-aunt Mabel, Tony caught the attention of Whacker and his dad and asked what the verdicts were on the drum set and the coach.

'Well,' said Ted, Whacker's dad, taking what seemed like the easiest bit of the question first, 'the lad's making a good job of cleaning and tuning the drums, and I'd like to see him able to finish the job off. We've got the space at home for him to do that, but not for him to set it all up and to play. On top of that, I'm sure the group don't need a full set, but it would be a shame to split it up.'

'Look,' said Tony, 'I meant what I said to Whacker. I'm more than pleased for all the drums to go, just to give me one less thing to decide what to do with. Take them with pleasure and do as you like with them. If the lads think they'll only ever need a few, then get rid of the rest any way you like. I've had them on my hands for ages, doing no good, nobody wanting them and me with enough other things to deal with. Sorry, I'm going on a bit, and round in circles as well, but I hope you'll believe me – I only hope you don't feel I'm trying to palm them off on you.'

'Thanks very much – that's really great. I'll take them home in the car today – if I can get the passengers in as well! Now, about the coach, that's a bit of a weird one. There's a brake shoe locked on one of the back wheels and I can't see why, or what's holding it there. So, there's no way it can just be towed out, and even without the brake problem the axles are probably solid – trying to move it without getting them lubricated could cause real problems. I just can't see how to deal with it, but, if it stays inside like it is now, I can't see how it can be checked over and fixed – it's a real problem.'

'I know I keep saying I've got enough things to deal with, but that coach intrigues me,' said Tony. 'If I found a way to move it out into the yard, could you then have a look at it for me? It won't be this weekend but I'd make it worth your while to come back some time.'

'I'd love to come and have a look but, as I say, at least one of the back wheels has a brake on, so that would have to be dealt with before even the strongest tractor could move it.'

'Let me think about it... I've still got some transport connections and I'm sure at least one of the guys will have an idea or two. Before you go I'll see if I can get hold of somebody – OK?'

'Yes, that's fine by me. The coach overall looks to be in decent nick, so it'll be well worth a bit of effort.'

The conversation seemed to be ending there, so Whacker chimed in, 'Did you get my dad to look at those pieces of furniture in the other coach house, Mr Philips?'

'Sorry, lad, I got too tied up with everything else. Why don't you take him down there when you're clear of here – and take the ladies too, they might be interested in some of the fabric things. You know where the key is.' And he moved off to have a word with the oldest couple there who really had had a day's worth of excitement and chat, and were showing signs of being ready to be on their way home.

As Ted and Whacker walked off to the stable block, Ted couldn't help commenting on his son's friendship with Tony Philips. 'He seems to have really taken to you, my lad, treating you almost like a son – how did that happen? I hope there's nothing more to it than that.'

'Give over, Dad,' he replied. 'I just happen to be more interested in his coach and other stuff than Boots and Slim are. Slim totally confused him talking his usual blah about our music, and Boots is more interested in his daughter, like I guess you noticed. And, of course, I was the first one to meet him and we had quite a chat before the others arrived.'

'What did you have to chat about, apart from the drums and your music?'

'Oh, he was telling me how he came to buy this place after his marriage broke up. I can't remember if he said as much, but I think he was wondering if he'd made a big mistake buying it.'

'So, he's not been here all his life, then? Oh, no, of course not, or he'd know all about the coach. So how come he bought it, the house I mean? Come up on the lottery or something? He certainly doesn't seem like the type that's born to money.'

'No, he sold most of a business – transport and scrap metal, I think he said. And from not too far away, I guess – his daughter still sees old friends. Actually, Dad, you and him don't seem very different, really. P'raps that's why we found it easy to chat.'

At this point they'd reached the stable yard, Whacker picked up the key and opened the coach house where the drum kit had been found.

'What's all this then?' asked Ted. 'And why should I be interested?'

'Give us a chance, Dad, I reckon I know what I'm doin'. Just give us a hand moving these sheets and cloths and you'll see.'

Removing the first couple of cloths only revealed an iron bedstead, some kitchen cabinets, an old fridge and so on. Moving behind these they lifted off some proper decorators' dust sheets and there was what Whacker had wanted his dad to see – sideboards, small cabinets, tables, two or three sorts of chairs and odds and ends of furniture, all in wood and some with different amounts, styles and conditions of upholstery.

'What a collection! But where did it all come from, and where do I come in?'

'I think most of this lot came from the houses here – that's the main house and the cottage across the yard that Tony's living in just now. The whole place was sold as it stood and he just moved stuff here while he had work done inside –

bits of plumbing and electrics and so on. When we get further back, I think there's stuff he brought with him.'

'It sounds like the whole process was a bit shambolic. Has he been ill or something? I can't see how you'd buy a place and not know it's furnished and then bring even more stuff! I mean, if he didn't have this storage place it'd be... I don't know what.' Ted paused, looked again at the mass of apparently fine furniture, and asked, 'What does he want me to do with it, anyway?'

'Well, Dad, I just said you'd like to see it, like you usually do at country houses and auctions and so on, and he said he'd like your opinion about it. You know – is it worth keeping or doing up or selling. I think he's just a bit overwhelmed by it all and honestly, he doesn't really know where to start. He's a nice bloke, Dad, and it would be great if you could help him out – it'd more than make up for him giving us the drum kit.'

'There's not much I can do today, you know, but he wants me to come back and look at the coach, so I'll see what time we have then – how's that? But for starters, that dressing table looks very much like a Waring and Gillow piece I saw in a catalogue last month – so, yes, I'll have a better look next time. Let's cover it up again and get back to see how your mum and Mrs Clark are getting on. Then I'll need you to give a hand getting some drums into the car, some now and the rest, I hope, when I come to look at the coach.'

Back at the house they found that most of the barbecue guests were now in the process of saying their goodbyes and getting ready to leave. Boots and Whacker were included in some of these, even though some of the older guests didn't really know who they were nor why they'd been included. Whacker's mum, Alison, and Boots' mum, Pauline, had been far more evident and involved in things, so their farewells were more heartfelt. But none were as fond as those for the birthday girl Anna, and (her assumed boyfriend) Boots – introduced here as John.

With the last of the other guests departed and the caterers dealt with, Tony suggested they all at last relax with a cup of tea, or whatever took their fancy, and a piece of cake – '*Please help us eat the cake or I'll be as fat as a house side!*'

And he insisted on getting the drinks himself – 'Come and sit yourselves down, Mr and Mrs W – I don't know how I'd have managed without you, so you'll have to think how I can repay you.' Then he turned his words into actions, took all their drinks orders and went off to prepare them, with Anna hot on his heels, and Boots not far behind.

Looking around, Pauline Clark asked, 'Where's Peter? I've just realised I've not seen him today. Is he OK?'

After exchanging puzzled looks, Mrs W asked, 'Who's Peter? I'm sure I've not met anybody of that name this weekend.'

Whacker laughed as he said, 'Oh yes you have, that's Slim's Sunday best name – but you've got me wondering now, Mrs C.'

'You lads and your nicknames! What's wrong with the names your parents gave you?'

Whacker's mum, Alison, took the boys' side with a smile, 'I guess we're as much to blame as the lads. Steven here has been known as Whacker since he was big enough to whack everything he laid hands on, but little did we know he'd develop into a drummer – and not a bad one at that, if I may say so.'

'Give over, Mum! We'll not see how good I am until we get this kit home and set up. Then I'll have to ask Mr Franks at school if he can give me a bit of tuition, and then see.'

'But you've still not said where Peter – or should I say, Slim – is. Is he all right? Or does he just feel out of it with his mum not able to be here?'

'He's fine, Mrs C. I don't know exactly where he is, but he went off on some sleuthing errand. He got chatting to a policeman that lives in the village, and I think he's trying to impress him in the hope of getting some tips on getting into the police.'

'Why ever would he do that when he's on holiday, and leave you two to fend for yourselves?' asked Whacker's mum, Alison.

Whacker couldn't help but laugh at his mum's idea that Slim sort of looked after him and Boots. Though he had to admit that it was Slim and his mum who'd done all the arranging for the weekend.

'He wouldn't have gone off if we'd been playing a gig today, and I'm pretty sure he wouldn't if we'd been backpacking. No, it just started when he found out that this chap having a drink in the pub on Friday evening was a police detective who lives in the village. He went to chat him up about joining the police and found he was working on a case of some local burglaries. Slim must have got some ideas about it and thinks it'll look good on his application to join if he helps solve the problem. I guess that's where he's off to this afternoon.'

'I do hope he's careful and doesn't get into a fight or something,' said Mrs Clark, 'you hear some terrible things about these gangs!'

'Don't worry, Mrs Clark, Slim's no hero. In fact, it's hard to imagine him in the police at all. Maybe this experience will help him get it out of his system. He's probably up at the inn licking his wounds and deciding how to tell us about it!'

At this point Tony and helpers returned with teapots and coffee jugs, with cups and mugs to suit. When everyone had been served and settled, Whacker just had to put a question that had been bothering him a bit.

'Just realised, Anna,' he said, 'where are the rest of your friends? Hope we didn't frighten them off?'

'Oh yes, you met the Alphabet Gang on Friday afternoon, didn't you?' interjected Tony.

'Dad! Don't be so mean! They're my friends and they're nice girls.'

'Of course they are. I'm just joking, love, but it's an easy way to remember them, you must admit – at least it is for me.'

Everybody else looked totally confused, causing Tony to explain, 'The girls are usually referred to in alphabetical order – Anna, Bel, Clare, and Deborah or Debs – so I just think of them as the Alphabet Gang. Though it sounds as if I'd best not let them hear me – right, Anna?'

'Don't worry, Dad, they'd not forsake me if they did. In fact, they might enjoy having a group name – I'll suss it out and let you know. Anyway, to answer your question, Whacker, Bel was here with her mum but had to leave early, and Clare and Debs left after the party last night; they had to get home for some family thing this morning. And no, I don't think you frightened them!'

In a bid to break the almost awkward silence, Whacker's dad, Ted, jumped in with – 'The lad tells me you've sold up your business to move here, Tony, so is that early retirement or are you planning to set something else up?'

'Ted!! You can't go asking people personal questions like that! Whatever will Mr Philips think of us?'

'It's all right – er, it is Alison isn't it? It's no secret that I sold up to get this place and, yes, as I was telling your lad yesterday, I'll need to get something going here. If I'm to stay it'll need to pay its way – but I must admit I can't imagine what it'll be.'

The ladies and Anna all looked a bit shocked at this. It was a lovely house, though needing a fair bit of its furnishings and décor sorting out, and none of them could imagine having to give it up if they lived there.

'Sorry to pour a bit of cold water on the weekend, Anna, but I've got to face facts. When you're not here, I'm rolling round like a pea in a drum. That's really why I've stayed in the staff cottage even after all the work in the big house had been done. But,' brightening up, 'I'm happy to consider anyone's ideas. Now don't let your tea grow cold and please DO help us make inroads into all the cake!'

Conversation stopped while they all tucked into the cakes and washed them down, but you could almost see them all thinking, mainly, 'What I'd give to have that sort of problem – why, I'd...'

Again, it was Ted who was the first to speak up. 'If you really want ideas, I must say I'd love to have my workshop here instead of the unit I've got in Bracknell. It's in an industrial estate and a bit soulless. I guess others would love it here, too, so you could set up the buildings in the stable yard as craft workshops, perhaps.'

Ted's wife didn't look too surprised at this; his unit really wasn't in a very nice location, but at least the area was secure, well managed, and not far from home. No, she decided, Ted might like the idea of a workshop here, but he'd never think seriously of the family moving out into the country, would he?

'OK, Ted, but are there enough craft people in the area wanting workshops? They'd have to live near enough to travel in every day, and it's not a type of business I'm familiar with so I wouldn't know what best to provide. They'd need toilets and cooking facilities for themselves – and even more of that if they had customers visiting. That's much more than I could run to with the balance of my savings, and I'm not sure there's the space for them, either.'

'Fair enough, Tony, but what about the stables? They must be complete, so no fitting-out to do there. Could you bring them into use at all?'

'Yes, Dad,' jumped in Anna, 'you did say something about me taking up horse riding. So, could I have a horse or a pony now I'm over sixteen?'

'Well that was part of the picture I had in mind, love, but I was really thinking of you in a riding school or a club or something. We've no experience of horses, so we couldn't just start like that from nothing.'

'I agree with you there, Tony,' joined in Ted again, 'but you could get advice, I'm sure.'

Boots' mum, Pauline, saw something of an answer. 'If you lived in the big house, you could rent out the smaller one to anybody wanting to use the other buildings, then they wouldn't be travelling in every day. And that would be an extra source of income.'

'Yes, but even if I could cope with all that space on my own, how many people would it take to look after it properly – the big house, I mean?'

'Four,' came the replies, almost in unison, from the Wilkinsons.

'Of course, I'd forgotten you both worked here. So, who would these people be?' asked Tony, privately quite interested in the idea.

'You go first, love,' said Mr W, 'you saw more of the inside workings than I did.'

'Right, assuming you took little or no part in the running of the household, Mr Philips, but concentrated on business interests, you'd need a housekeeper to run things and do odds and ends to fill gaps, then you'd need a cook, then a maid or cleaner, and finally a man to do heavy lifting, gardening, odd jobs and possibly some driving to collect shopping and such. So really, you'd also probably need some backups to call on to cover holidays and sickness.'

'Don't forget the laundry, love,' added Mr W.

'Oh yes. If you were the only one living in, sir, laundry could be done between the maid, housekeeper and cook. But when you had guests, and perhaps if any of the staff were living in, you'd have to send some of it, perhaps even all of it, to a laundry.'

'Wow!' said Tony. 'Is that what my wife coped with, on her own?'

'It's what every wife copes with, Mr Philips!' replied Mrs W, smiling to show it wasn't a criticism. 'Unless she gets help from her husband. And it does help if the children,' looking at the lads and Anna in turn, 'at least keep their bedrooms tidy.' (*Hint to young readers!!*)

At this last comment, Anna surprised them all by flinging herself into her dad's arms and bursting out crying, 'Daddy, I'm so sorry, so, so very, very sorry!'

'There, there, my love. Don't upset yourself so. What's brought this on?'

'It's because of me that Mum left us, isn't it? I just didn't do anything to help at home; at least I didn't do enough. And what Mrs Wilkinson just said made me realise it and how much I miss her and she doesn't miss me and she didn't come to my birthday party and she's horrid.' All this interspersed with sobs and sniffles, as all of Anna's pent-up, probably unrecognised, feelings caused by the break-up of her parents' marriage gushed out.

The others turned to each other and tried to start conversations that would allow Anna and Tony to have some privacy. The lads really wanted to move away, but Mr W asked Whacker how he was getting on with the drums, Ted joined in with his plans for getting them home, and it all allowed Anna to regain her composure.

'I'm so sorry for that,' she said, drying her eyes and going back to her seat next to Boots. 'I didn't know I could still be such a baby. And please don't tell my friends – the Alphabet Gang!!' ending with a giggle.

'Don't you worry, my dear,' responded Mrs W. 'It's been an exciting weekend for you and it's come at the end of a spell of great change. It's understandable that your emotions have been all over the place, but you have a lovely future ahead of you, I'm sure.'

All the chat about plans for the future was brought to an end by the ringing of the phone in the entrance hall of the main house. Tony jumped up and went in to answer it, looking slightly annoyed at the interruption, but he was back in a moment calling for Anna to go and join him. As she approached, he mouthed over her head to the others that it was her mother, and smiled.

* * *

Some time earlier, out on the Salchester road, Slim thanked a silent Mr West as he got out of the car outside the kennels.

'Could you give me a lift back, please, if I'm across the road?'

'Yup.'

'Thanks again Mr West.'

'Yup. And don't forget to ask them to microchip you, my lad!' and his laugh followed him as he drove off.

Slim had visited a couple of kennels the day before and found there was no typical building for them, and this one followed the same lack of pattern. It was just a country cottage that identified itself as Skelford Kennels and Cattery by means of a fairly discrete sign saying that it was open 8 a.m. to 6 p.m., please ring for attention. So Slim did as he was bid.

Nothing seemed to happen and he wondered how long to wait before ringing again. Then he heard a couple of dogs barking, followed by the sound of footsteps approaching along the gravel path that led around the side of the cottage. The young girl – about his own age, he guessed – who appeared leading an elderly Labrador, stopped in surprise on seeing Slim waiting by the door.

'You're obviously not Mrs Smithers, but did she send you?' she asked.

'Not guilty,' replied Slim, 'and I'm not here to collect any animal, thanks. I just wanted a bit of info about your services, charges and so on, if that's OK on a Sunday.'

'Of course, no problem. If you'd like to hang on a minute in the office I'll take Sammy into the back until Mrs Smithers arrives.' So saying, she unlocked and opened the cottage front door and led Slim inside.

What had once been a wide entrance hall was fitted with a waist-high reception counter that separated the customers from the office area. The girl led the dog through to a door that opened into a passage and they disappeared from view.

Wasting no time, Slim stepped forward, leaned over the counter and studied the diary-cum-bookings register that lay open on the desk behind it. Of course, it was opened at the current week but he quickly flipped a few pages back and Bingo! There, on succeeding lines, two of the addresses that he'd memorised were booked in, and for the dates when they'd been burgled!

The feeling of success evaporated in an instant when he sensed, as much as heard, the front door opening behind him. He turned to find a very angry-looking youth, a lot bigger than himself, taking the two steps that brought him right into Slim's face.

'What you think you're doin' 'ere, mate? You botherin' my girl?'

Slim could only open his mouth in indignation before he felt a hard jab to his midriff that knocked the air out of him with a whoosh. Then, before he could even think of doing or trying to say anything in response, he took a hard punch to the jaw. The last thing he heard before he passed out and slumped to the floor was a piercing scream from the girl who'd seen the blow as she came back into the room.

'What on earth do you think you're doing, Jerry, you THUG? What have you done to him? Is he OK?' All this at the top of her voice and clearly heard out in the road through the door that the yob had left open.

'Shut up, stupid! I was protecting you, OK?'

Needless to say, that didn't go down well, and it didn't calm her or stop her pushing him out through the door.

By this time Slim was recovering a bit. He'd never been in that state before and didn't know what was best to do – stay on the floor a bit longer, or get up and try to shrug it off. The girl made the decision for him.

'You stay there a minute, sir. I'm calling the boss, she's a first-aider.' So saying, she used an intercom and asked whoever replied to bring a first aid kit to reception. Looking up, she was pleased to see that the attacker had beaten a hasty retreat out of the building and was walking briskly along the road towards town. She also noticed a small open-topped car parked a few yards along the road. But she didn't know that the driver had stopped only when he'd heard the shouting and fighting, and had called the police.

CHAPTER 12

Back at the Manor House only a few items of patio furniture remained outside. Tony had rejoined the others after about ten minutes, explaining that Anna had had a heart-to-heart chat with her mum and was now getting changed. They had all then pitched in to get things back to what they felt was normal.

The atmosphere was of a typical summer Sunday evening – quiet, almost sleepy. Amongst the people there was that air that always exists between visitors and hosts towards the end of a visit – 'Should we be going now?' 'How do I get them to start leaving?'

Here it was Whacker's dad, Ted, who broke the stalemate almost simultaneously with the host, Tony – 'I had a quick look at...' 'Did you manage to look at...' and they both stopped and everyone laughed.

'You first, Ted, OK?'

'Right, I did have a quick look, but only at the front part of the – dare I call it a pile? I don't know about the chairs, but there was a dressing table looking very like a Waring and Gillow piece I've seen in an auction catalogue.'

'I think I know the one you mean,' interrupted Mrs W, 'and if I'm right, it was the mistress's favourite – from the main bedroom.'

'I must admit I can't remember where all the pieces came from,' said Tony. 'I suppose I should have labelled them, but I had no real idea what I'd eventually want to do with it all. Does it look in good nick, Ted?'

'Yes, from where I stood, but I'd need to be able to look at it closely. You sometimes find wear and tear to the moving parts – drawers and hinges – and that's usually easily fixed, but surface damage can be a problem. I'll have a look if there's time when I come back to see the carriage, if you like.'

'That'd be great, I'd really appreciate your opinion – any idea how long you'd need?'

'As long as a piece of string, really. You'd best tell me your priorities and I'll get done as much as poss.'

'Well, for me the carriage comes first as it's taking up all that space, so I'll get a mechanic over to see what we can do to move it. When that's organised, I can give you a bell and take it from there to fit in with your other commitments, OK?'

'Fine.'

With that topic settled, Mrs W jumped in. 'If you don't mind me asking, sir, sorry – Mr Philips – do you intend to put the good furniture back where it came from?'

'I hadn't really thought about it, but I suppose that's as good an idea as any – except that I can't really remember where most of it did come from – you couldn't write me some notes before you move on, could you, please?'

'Oh gosh, that's asking something! We're not the best writers in the world, but we're not moving on just yet, so we could come along and have another look with you, if you'd like – but do say when we look like becoming a nuisance, won't you?' she ended rather anxiously, never before having spoken like that to someone she considered to be her employer.

'From what you know of this place and how it used to be, I can't ever see you two becoming nuisances – in fact, if you lived round here I'm sure you'd find me being the nuisance!'

'Well, if that's the case,' joined in Mr W, 'we've got no firm plans to move on so, if they can let us stay on a bit longer at the Red Lion, we'd be happy to do that. Would you like us to look into it?'

'That'd be terrific but, if you're here to help me, we'll have to work out how I can repay you – same for you on the carriage and furniture, Ted, OK?'

They all saw he was serious about it, so didn't argue, though each of them felt that the chance to be there and deal with things they loved was reward enough.

'Now we seem to have things settled,' Tony continued, 'let's get these lads back to the Red Lion, check what their pal's been up to, and I'll get us all some supper, OK?'

But, back at the Red Lion, there was no sign of Slim and no message from him. Tina had seen Mr Rogers after he'd come back from Salchester and asked about Slim.

'Did you get him there OK?'

'Yup.'

'Was he there to be picked up when you came back?'

'Nope.'

'Did you see him anywhere around there when you drove past?'

'Nope. There was just a police car.'

That was all she could tell the others when they arrived from the Manor, and it didn't sound good to Boots and Whacker, or their parents – but what could they do? Tina's dad then came in and offered to ring the police and ask about Slim. He, Jim, felt something of a responsibility for his guests, particularly young people who'd been sort of entrusted into his care.

Coming back from the office, he told them he'd rung the home of the officer that lived in the village, but that the phone was engaged.

The phone in question had only just rung in the home of DC 'Loada' Cole. His wife answered it to find the caller was their friend Harry Collins, a sergeant based in Salchester. She'd assumed it was a social call and had started to ask about Harry's wife and children when he gently interrupted and said he needed to speak to DC Cole on a police matter, so she called him and handed the phone over.

'DC Cole, Sarge, what can I do for you?'

'Just what you might call a bit of babysitting, Loada. We've got a young chap here says he's staying at the Red Lion in the village and that he knows you – lad by the name of Peter Bennett, but you might know him as Slim. Ring any bells?'

'Well, if it's who I think it is, I had a word with him on Friday in the Lion, or should I say, he had a word with me! Wants to join the force and wanted to know about our local burglaries – that the one?'

'Yes, that's him all right.'

'So, what's he done to get your undivided attention, Sarge? Solved it all, has he?' and they both had a good chuckle at that idea.

'No, but not for want of trying, and he may have given us a lead worth pursuing, but for heaven's sake don't tell him that!'

'OK, so what's happening? What do you want me to do?'

'Well, we were called to a dust-up at Skelford Kennels this afternoon and found matey with bruised ribs, a sore jaw, and feeling sorry for himself. The girl on duty there said he'd been attacked by none other than our old friend Jerry Doyle.'

'He must be pressing charges, then, is he?'

'Not at all. The girl says she'd love to see him charged. Doyle's been pestering her and, according to our lad, what Doyle said when he hit him was something like, "Keep away from my girl". BUT, when we got the lad to the station to make a statement, he told us this tale about chatting to you, and looking for clues on these burglaries. With me so far, Loada?'

'I think so, Sarge.'

'Right. Well it seems he was looking at the kennel's diary when Doyle hit him, and he'd managed to see that a couple of the burgled families had their dogs booked in at the kennels while they were on holiday.'

'Yes, we knew that, Sarge, but we couldn't see how that helped, could we? So what's new?'

'Well, our laddie, Slim Whatsisname, managed to see those bookings by looking over the reception counter, right? – so we have to consider the possibility that our burglar could have done that as well. BUT, don't you think it's interesting that we've found Jerry Doyle sniffing around the girl that works there? We don't reckon Doyle's got the nous to do the jobs himself, but he's probably being used by one of his contacts. Anyway, the outcome is that we ignore this little scrap and send young Slim home – for the moment, anyway. But who knows how things might develop, and somebody may need him back if things mature and get to court.'

'So why do you need me to look after him, Sarge? Him and his mates are here under their own steam, after all.'

'Oh, it's just precautionary on two counts, really. First off, we had the medic take a look at him as he'd been knocked out, so we need the people at the place he's staying to be aware of it in case anything develops overnight – *in loco parentis*, if they know what that means! Secondly, if Doyle or his buddies are involved, we don't want them finding him before he leaves and persuading him to see things their way. We'll get in touch with our colleagues in Bracknell to put them in the picture if things develop that way – you never know, we might have just got lucky.'

'OK, Sarge, I'll see he's tucked up safely in his little bed at the Red Lion tonight.'

'Knew you'd see it my way, Loada. Goes without saying I want you to walk him to the Lion – one of our patrol cars'd really give the game away if Doyle or any of his buddies are keeping tabs on things. Anyway, the car should be outside your house any minute now!' And Loada was sure he heard him laugh before the phone went down.

He quickly got his shoes and coat on while explaining things to his wife, and had his front door open just as the patrol car pulled up outside. He greeted Slim as he climbed out, waved the car off, then took Slim's arm to lead him straight to the Red Lion. On the way there, he explained only that they were concerned for his health and that the landlord at the Red Lion needed to be aware of his injuries.

'No,' he reassured him, 'the police doctor was quite happy that you'll be OK, but we'd do just the same if we were taking you home to your family – the people you're staying with just need to know, that's all. Anyway, all we tell them about what happened is that you were going towards Salchester and were the victim of an unprovoked attack. It was reported to the police who are looking into it, and the police doctor gave you some painkillers. Best not to say what you were really doing or they'll just keep asking questions instead of letting you get to bed for a good sleep. OK, son?'

'Yes, but I found out how they could have done it, didn't I?'

'We'll have to wait and see, son. It's not something new and our enquiries are continuing. As I say, and this comes from HQ in the city, if anybody asks, you were on your way to the city for a look round, OK?'

Slim's reply – 'Yes, I guess so.' – indicated how tired and ready for bed he was, and their arrival became a muted affair after Loada gave the agreed explanation and asked for Slim to be given chance for a good night's sleep.

When he got the landlord on his own, Loada asked him to let them know at HQ – he gave him the number to use – once Slim was safely on the bus on his way home. He didn't tell him that that call would result in another one being made to the police HQ in Bracknell for them to look out for the lad.

Chapter 13

After escorting Slim upstairs, Boots and Whacker were far from ready for bed themselves and were soon back in the Residents' Lounge with their parents, and Tony, Anna, and the Wilkinsons. This time, on neutral ground, folk wanted to carry on talking about the day they'd had and about thoughts for the future.

It was clear to all that Boots and Whacker wanted to stay in the village a bit longer or, more precisely, to spend time around the Manor. Boots' main aim – of staying close to Anna – was not mentioned. As for Whacker, he was in no doubt that it would at least help his dad if he could do a bit of preliminary sorting of the furniture that Tony wanted him to look at in the coach house. Both his dad and Tony had realised that not much furniture could be properly scrutinised unless it was in the open, and both had wondered about how to get it done without bringing in a couple of labourers.

So, after a nod of agreement between himself and Tony, Ted went to have a word with landlord Jim. When he found that the lads could stay on in their room until Thursday, or even Friday if necessary, he booked them in for the full week and made arrangements for some of their laundry to be dealt with.

With things looking a lot clearer, Mrs W felt confident enough to speak up about what should eventually be done with the furniture. She suggested that, unless Tony had other strong ideas, the pieces might best be replaced where they used to be when the family lived there and before they had to be moved to make way for repairs and modernising and so on. By this time, Whacker and Boots were being seen as the removal men but, if they realised it, it didn't bother them – there'd be plenty time for things they wanted to do.

'I suppose,' said Tony, 'if we get the furniture back roughly where it came from, the whole place will look more like a home than a building site. But even then, I can't see me living in it on my own, as I would be when you're away, Anna.'

'Come on, Dad,' she replied, rather woefully. 'Surely you'd be able to find somebody to help out with the cleaning, and you can always eat out and send clothes to the laundry. I mean, if you take to living in the small house all the time, then won't the big house just get in the state it was when you bought it? And all that work'll have been a waste of money! And what do I tell my friends about where we live?' She was almost on the verge of tears again as she ran out of things to say to try to persuade him to change his mind.

'Don't get in a state, love, it's not like I'm suggesting I sleep outside somewhere. But you must realise a house that big was meant for a family with staff to look after it – and to look after them. And I don't really regret buying it. I suppose the real problem is that I haven't yet worked out how I'm going to occupy myself – I reckon once I've sorted that out I'll see clearer how to use the house. Until then, I'm finding it easier to live in the cottage and not let the situation of the big house occupy too much of my thoughts. OK?'

But Anna wasn't prepared to let it drop, like that. She imagined her dad would just carry on living in the staff cottage and give no thought to the Manor House apart from getting the furniture put back in.

'Mrs Wilkinson,' she asked, 'how many people would it take to look after the house the way it used to be, but with just Dad and sometimes me living in it?'

'Oh, my dear,' she replied, rather taken aback with such a forthright question, and not wanting to interfere in a family dispute. 'All I can tell you is what the situation was when Mr W and I worked here.'

'That's fine. It will give us something concrete to base our ideas on – make it more like one of the problems our maths teacher often comes up with. OK, Dad?'

'Of course, love. At least Mr and Mrs Wilkinson are unbiased in this.'

Mr and Mrs W had been quietly comparing notes and ticking things off on their fingers during Tony and Anna's exchange, and Mrs W was ready to start.

'Well, first off, the staff situation was, of course, geared to suit the family. When I was first here there were two children of school age and they had a nanny and sometimes a tutor, but I think we can discount those. So, there was a housekeeper, a cook, a butler-cum-valet, a cleaning maid, a general maid and a chauffeur, so that's six, BUT...'

'Wait a minute, though, that's at least a couple more than you quoted that I'd need, the last time it was raised, so why the difference? Is it something that's going to sneak up and bite me?'

'No, worry not, Mr Philips,' with a smile. 'First off, you'd not be needing all the rooms in the house – you'd just have to decide which ones to use. The rest would be kept as what we used to call Sunday best – ready for use, but not needing daily cleaning. With that set-up, and depending on how much you'd want to join in and help with the likes of shopping and gardening, you'd be able to manage with just a couple of staff – they'd mainly do cooking and cleaning. How does that sound?'

But it was Anna who jumped in. 'Sounds fine to me, Mrs. W, and I'd do my bit when I'm at home, so that wouldn't need any extra staff. So, does it all sound a bit better now, Dad?'

When Tony nodded a tentative yes, Anna waded in again. 'So, could you come and work in the house for Dad, please, Mr and Mrs W?'

There was an all-round shocked silence.

Tony's features blackened like thunder – 'ANNA! How dare you even think that of our guests! Don't you realise that everything that Mr and Mrs Wilkinson have done for us over this weekend has taken time out of their valuable holiday plans? After you've apologised we'd better get you home!'

Anna, of course, had not meant to upset anyone. She was quite sure in her own mind that the Wilkinsons had loved every minute of being back where they'd met, and she felt sure she'd only said what they, and perhaps even her dad, had begun to think. But she'd never seen her dad so angry, not even when her mum had broached the subject of divorce so, hanging her head to hide her emerging tears, she said, 'I'm so sorry, Mr and Mrs W. It just feels so right you being in the house and I just got carried away. Please forgive me, and PLEASE don't be annoyed with Dad.'

Mrs Wilkinson had to choke back her own tears, realising the depth of feeling that was behind Anna's outburst and apology, and it took her a moment or two to smile and reply. 'Of course we're not annoyed with you Anna, are we Harry? It's very touching that you feel that way about us and that you're trying so hard to help your father. But these really are his decisions to make.'

Looking at his watch, Whacker's dad started to get up, saying, 'Didn't realise it was getting as late as this, so we'd best be off. We'll see you Wednesday or Thursday depending, OK, Tony? And,' with a grin, 'don't work these lads too hard or we'll have them off school claiming they need a rest.'

'What do you mean, Dad? We'll be on the bus home in the morning.'

'Oh?' with mock severity. 'Didn't I tell you we've booked you both in to stay here until I come back to see the coach and furniture? Both of you are Mr Philips's labour force to get the furniture moved back into the house and put where Mr and Mrs W say it should go! And no slacking!!'

The big grins that appeared on Boots' and Whacker's faces showed that the prospect of hard work was no problem if they could stay around the Manor House (not to mention a couple of young ladies!) for a few more days.

'But, Dad,' started Whacker, 'we didn't bring any spare clothes!'

'Now there's a first!' laughed his mum. 'Our Whacker worrying about having clean clothes to change into! Don't worry, my lad, the landlord will deal with it for you – all taken care of.'

By this time, they were all – Tony and Anna, the Wilkinsons, Boots, Whacker, and their parents – heading out towards the door and the car park. Tina followed and, in asking the two mums if there were any special instructions for washing their sons' clothes, made the good impression that her father had always insisted on when dealing with current, and potential, guests.

Once the carload of parents had set off for home in Bracknell, Tony and Anna bade the others goodnight and set off for the Manor House, then the Wilkinsons said their goodnights and headed for bed. It was only just dark and still warm, so Whacker and Boots settled for a relax and a chat at one of the benches in the Red Lion's beer garden. Tina came out to clear some tables, and turned to walk back inside but joined them when Whacker called her over.

'Look, Tina,' he started, 'Dad says he's booked me and Boots, here, to stay on more or less for the rest of the week, but he never mentioned Slim. What's the situation there? Is he staying as well, cos if not, he's not going to be a happy bunny.'

'Oh no,' she replied, 'it's only you two staying. Your dad did ask about your friend, but he couldn't have extended his stay, anyway, as that room, and all the others, are already booked for the rest of the month. Is it going to be a real problem for him, going home on his own?'

'Course not – he's just going to feel a bit put out, that's all. You see, Tina, he loves to act as our leader. For instance, this weekend was a joint idea, but he did all the organising, and the timing was to suit him – his mum was going to be away, so it saved him looking after himself or being dragged along to some history group or such!'

'If it's going to be a worry, I guess you'd better have a word with him first thing in the morning or it'll be a shock if the first he knows is when he's the only one on the bus!'

Boots and Whacker couldn't help a little chuckle at the image of Slim's THE PLAN ending that way, but sobered up when they saw Tina's look of disapproval.

'It might be more of a blow to him than you realise,' she said. 'Don't forget he got injured this afternoon and he could still be feeling the effects of it in the morning.'

'Sorry, love – oops – Tina,' stammered Whacker. 'In all our talk tonight, I'd sort of forgotten Slim's problem. What was it again?'

'We don't know much, really. All Mr Cole said was that he'd been attacked in the street, somebody called the police, their doctor had a look at him, he told them what had happened, and he needs a good night's sleep.'

'Thanks, Tina. I'm sure it's as they said – Slim wouldn't have started anything – you're not harbouring Berkshire criminals.'

'Never thought we were,' with a smile. 'Now, if you'll excuse me, I've got an early start tomorrow helping with breakfasts for hungry guests.'

Chapter 14

Monday morning found Boots and Whacker already sitting down to breakfast before Slim appeared, looking a bit bruised and still a bit sleepy.

'What got you two up so early, then? Bet you're not packed, are you?' he asked sitting down rather gingerly.

'Well, no, Slim. We're staying on for a few days, helping out at the house, you know.'

Slim, of course, didn't know and wasn't sure he believed him – Whacker loved to pull legs – but decided to let it pass, he was a bit too fragile to join in his games.

'Right,' he said. 'Well I'm all ready for the off, so I'll see you outside about ten past just in case it's a bit early.'

Boots realised Slim really had no idea what was happening so decided that it was about time they set things straight.

'Look, Slim, we're sorry to send you off on your own, right, but it was a bit of a last-minute decision and you weren't around and your room's already booked for the rest of the week, and, well...' he petered out.

But Slim was concentrating on his breakfast and wasn't really looking and listening. If he had been, he would have realised that Boots was serious, as was Whacker for a change.

'Yes, fine,' he said, without looking up. 'See you outside at ten past.'

Boots and Whacker looked at each other wondering if the attack he'd sustained had caused Slim any real major damage. But realising there was nothing else they could do, they got up from the table, said 'Cheerio', went up to their room, cleaned their teeth, sorted out their laundry and set off for the Manor House.

And so it was that, when the bus arrived at 9.15, only Slim and a couple of ladies off to do some shopping were at the stop outside the Post Office. Still thinking the lads were pulling his leg, Slim climbed aboard, stowed his guitar case and bag in the luggage rack, and settled on the back seat to wait for the others to arrive.

But, of course, they didn't.

As the bus started to pull away, Slim jumped up and hammered his fists against the side window and started shouting, 'You sods!! You rotten sods!! You rotten bloody sods!!' Then fell to repeating, 'Rotten bloody sods!' again and again as the bus moved off with no sign of his pals anywhere. By this time, he was sobbing as he shouted, his face growing more and more red, his bruise from yesterday showing more and more.

His actions and his language initially offended the other passengers, all women from the village and most of them mothers. Then their maternal instincts kicked in as they recognised that here was someone's son, absolutely distraught as a result of someone else's actions, and they came to his aid. The one nearest the front rang the bell and called on the driver, Graham, to stop the bus, which he did.

'What's all this then, Agnes?' he asked.

'Why, can't you hear him up there, Graham? The poor lad's off his head with grief about something and he's in no condition to carry on, if you ask me.'

'What am I supposed to do about it, then? You know I've got a timetable to keep, and if he wants to get to Oxford on time I can't hang around for long. Who is he? Do you know?'

One of the women who had gone to sit with Slim was calming him down. 'Yes, his pals called him Slim, and he's been with them at the Lion this weekend. Looks like they're staying behind or something and he's been left to get home on his own. But I don't think he's in a fit state to carry on.'

Before the discussion could go any further, there was a knocking on the bus door and there was Graham's wife, Eileen, asking what was happening. When they told her and she stepped up into the bus, she recognised Slim from seeing him with his pals in the Red Lion on Friday when Boots did so well in Tell-a-Tale. After a career as a district nurse, Eileen felt sure that Slim should not continue his journey on his own in his present state.

'How far is he going, Graham?'

'With us, just as far as Oxford, but his full ticket is to Bracknell, changing to his local service at Reading. Why?'

'I reckon you should put him off for now and give him chance to get settled. Then he can go off on the 11 o'clock. You can give him a voucher for that, can't you?'

'Course I can, but starting at eleven will have him in the teatime crowd around Reading. Could he cope with that if he's not fully fit?'

'We can't tell, can we, but I don't think it's right to let him carry on right now. I reckon we'd best take him off and see how he is about half ten. In any case we ought to get in touch with his family, let them know what's happening. They may want to come and collect him.'

One of the other women asked where his pals were, anyway. If they really were his pals they ought to come and give a hand, particularly as their actions seemed to have started all this trouble.

That comment drew complete agreement, and a subdued Slim was led off the bus. His bag and guitar were collected for him and Graham did the necessary to show that Slim had not, after all, used his ticket to get from Charlford to Salchester.

Out on the footpath, Slim allowed Eileen to lead him back to the Red Lion where Jim and Tina were shocked when told what had happened. Tina was despatched to make him a cup of hot sweet tea, and to check that they still had his home phone number. But before she got any of that done, she was back to say that there was a call for Slim from his home.

Jim went in and took the call. 'Hello, this is Jim Parker. I'm the landlord of the Red Lion. How can I help?'

'Hello, Mr Parker. I told the young lady who answered the phone that I've got a message for Peter Bennett – if he hasn't set off already I'd like to speak to him. Oh, I should say I'm their neighbour and I'm calling on behalf of his mother. Tell him it's Mrs Harris.'

'Well he hasn't set off yet, Mrs Harris, but he can't come to the phone at the moment – can I give him a message?'

'Yes, if you would, please. You see, his mother had a doctor's appointment this morning and, quite unexpectedly I believe, they sent her to hospital in Reading to have some tests done and told her she'll be there until Wednesday afternoon. That means Peter will come home to an empty house and empty larder, so I'm offering him his meals until he gets sorted. But I'm calling now as I thought he'd want to call in and see his mum on his way through Reading. Er, sorry it's a bit rambling, but I suppose I'm a bit caught on the hop.'

'Don't worry about that, Mrs Harris, but I'm not sure when Peter will get home. You see, he had a bit of an accident yesterday and the local nurse isn't sure he's fit to travel yet. It was nothing to worry about, but it shook him up a bit. I reckon this sort of thing seems worse when you're away from home. Anyway, if you can give me your home number we can let you know what's happening, and Peter can perhaps give his mum a ring in hospital if he decides not to come home today. Is that all right, do you think?'

So Slim got his cup of tea and was told that things had been reported to his home, and that he was to relax and not think about travelling until he felt more settled and had sorted things out with his pals. Jim had spoken to Eileen and, between them, they had decided that they shouldn't yet pass on the information about his mother being in hospital.

'But,' said Jim, 'if he's not fit to travel today, I don't know where he's going to sleep – all my rooms are booked.'

'We'll worry about that if it happens,' replied Eileen. 'For now, I'd like to keep an eye on him so, if you agree, I'll take him with me on the library run – in fact, I ought to be off now, my regulars will think I've got a puncture or something.'

Leaving his bag and guitar in Jim's care, Eileen led Slim out to go find her mobile library. Taking a deep breath and squaring his shoulders, Slim asked her quietly, 'I suppose it's expecting too much to ask you not to broadcast what just happened?'

'Don't worry about those of us that just helped you, love, but you did choose a bit of a public arena for your event,' and smiled to take any sting out of it. Thankfully, though rather surprisingly, Slim gave a rueful smile. 'I think I'll blame it on being jumped on and getting beaten up – never happened to me before, and I hope it won't again, I tell you.'

Meanwhile, at the Manor House, Boots, Whacker and the Wilkinsons had gone straight to the stable yard and found Tony and Anna opening the first coach house door to reveal the heap of belongings covered mainly in dust sheets

'What's the plan, then, Mr Philips?' asked Mr W.

'That's what I'm just trying to decide. I go along with the idea of putting things back in the rooms they were in during your time here, but I'm not sure that all the pieces in each group came from the same room. So it's really a case of dealing with each item as we come to it and relying on your memory to say where it came from.' Pause for thought. 'In fact, I reckon that's the simplest anyway. Then young Whacker here can have a chance to look at each piece of furniture and decide if it might need his dad to have a closer look at it later this week. So, I'm afraid it looks as if it could get messy. What do you think, Mr W?'

'If Miss Anna could get hold of a notebook and some sticky labels, I think we could make a tidy job of it. All right, Miss?'

'That sounds fine to me,' she replied, 'particularly if it means I get a clean job!' And off she went to get the things from her school bag.

'My dad is only going to look at furniture, so pictures and rugs and such can go straight to their rooms, can't they? In fact, the floor coverings need to go down first anyway, so we could make a start with those, could we?'

'Ah, I should have mentioned,' said Tony. 'There's a cleaning company due here any time now to give a final overall clean of the bare rooms and then give the carpets a special cleaning before the furniture goes in. I'd better have a word with them and check if they want to do that with the carpets in situ. Can I leave you to be getting some of the dust covers off and I'll go and have a word with them – and chase them up if they're not here yet.'

About to set off, Tony paused as another thought occurred to him. 'Mr W, would you mind coming with me? I'm sure it'll help the cleaning people to know what sort of things go where, so we can sort out what to do first.' And off they both went, deep in conversation.

'You know,' said Boots, 'this suddenly doesn't look as straight forward as I thought.'

'Why's that then,' asked Whacker, 'you heard what the man said – get the covers off and …. Yeah, see what you mean. Where do we move stuff to?'

'Well, we need it all back in the house, don't we?' joined in Anna. 'And I'm going to put labels on things, and make lists and stuff, aren't I? Don't say I went and got the pens, and labels and paper all for nothing!'

'Don't get your feathers in a frizz, Miss Philips, you'll get to be the secretary bird soon enough,' joked Boots. 'Thing is, it's going to take more muscle than me and Whacker here to shift all this. So, until your dad says where he wants it, all we can really do is take a couple of covers off.'

'Well don't just stand there, do something! Then we can at least start labelling, and Whacker can tell me what sort of things he needs me to write down for his dad! Men!! Can't you do anything without being told?' But Anna giggled as she got them moving.

As the lads advanced on the front pile of things, Whacker made a quiet aside to Boots, 'You need to be careful with that one, you know. She'll have you doing the cleaning, the ironing and the washing up if you don't establish who's boss from the off!' and burst out laughing at Boots' blushing face.

'Don't know what you're talking about!'

'Aw, come on! Everybody's seen you trailing around after her like a little puppy dog. You know you fancy her like mad.'

'Well, what if I do? She's a lovely girl. And what about you and moonlit walks with the fair Tina? Didn't think we'd seen you, did you? Fancy your chances as a pub landlord, do you?' And gave Whacker a playful elbow in the ribs.

Secretly pleased that their amorous intentions were at last out in the open, the lads got on with the job in hand. They carefully removed and folded the dust sheets so as to avoid creating the clouds of dust that had accompanied their first foray into the task. Anna stuck a numbered label on each piece of furniture and wrote in the book what Whacker said it was and which room she thought it might go in.

They hadn't got very far when Tony returned driving a van and towing a small flatbed trailer.

'Right, folks. The cleaners want to do the carpets either outside, if it stays dry – and it looks like it will – or in the main hall. Quite rightly they don't want to be carrying dusty carpets into the rooms they've just cleaned – don't know why I didn't think of that myself!'

'Cos you're a bloke, Dad!' laughed Anna. 'Any female worth her salt could have told you that!'

'Enough cheek from you, young lady, or I'll send the cleaners away and have you doing it all!'

'Right, sir,' intervened Boots, 'what do we move out first? We reckon we'd best only do one heap at a time or we'll have a right shambles.'

'That's what I've come to say – we need to take any carpets for downstairs first, then they can be drying before being walked on, OK? After that they want the furniture and stuff a room at a time. We'll leave it in small groups in the hall so it can be cleaned up before it's moved to where it belongs. The Wilkinsons are on their way to help sort things out into room batches, so that's what you'll need to know for the labels, OK? They're bringing drinks as well, so we can have our morning break. I know it's a bit early, but I really do need their ideas on this and, anyway, the removal guys aren't here yet, so there's no real rush.'

'Come on, Dad! I know the Wilkinsons are being a great help, but surely it's our home and up to us where we put things?'

'It's certainly our house, but I'm still not sure it's going to be our home.'

That stopped them all in their tracks, including Mr and Mrs W who'd just arrived with a tray of drinks.

Whacker was the first to respond. 'Are you going to use it as a hotel then, Tony?'

'No, it's not big enough – at least it hasn't got enough bedrooms, but I reckon the ground floor would work OK.'

'So,' came in Boots, 'what about a B&B – there's enough rooms for that, aren't there?'

Tony couldn't help but laugh that all the ideas were coming from boys who probably had no more idea on running a home than he himself had!

'Look, I really do appreciate that you're trying to help, but I think I need to talk to somebody experienced in these sorts of businesses.'

That seemed to end the discussion so they found themselves seats and got stuck into the drinks and cakes the Wilkinsons had brought with them.

'Are you seriously thinking of a hotel or B&B, sir?' asked Mr W.

'At the moment, I don't honestly know what to think – I'm just hoping it will all become clearer once we've got the main house straight again. One thing's for sure, I'm beginning to realise what a large part a wife plays in running a home. I suppose because most of it's done when you're at work you just don't realise the effort, the knowledge and the planning that goes into it. Let that be a lesson to you young lads – don't take your mother, or later your wife, for granted. Get stuck in and give her a hand.' Another pause followed by a wry smile, 'Here endeth the lesson.'

'Golly, Dad, somebody ought to have told you all that before you lost Mum to that bloke – he's not half the man that you are, as she'll find out one day.'

'OK, Anna, but I think we've aired enough of our dirty linen for now. Let's get this room's-worth loaded and up to the house and see where to go from there.'

The Wilkinsons soon pointed out the items that had come from the main bedroom – dressing table, stools, pictures, wardrobe, tallboy, vases, blanket chests and such. The items and the carpets were carefully loaded and taken to the front door of the house ready to be moved upstairs after the carpets had been cleaned and laid again.

Realising it would be some time before another set of furniture could be moved, Tony decided they should look instead at the coach. Whacker had already opened the doors to reveal the coach and had brought out the towrope. Under Mr W's guidance he threaded one end of it through the ringbolt in the floor and then to the back wall and up through the ringbolt there.

While this was happening, Tony had uncoupled the trailer and reversed the van round ready to tow the coach out into the yard. Seeing what Whacker was doing, he got out of the van and interrupted the process with, 'I thought the elaborate rope trick was for getting the coach *back* into the building!' And they all laughed in embarrassment. 'But no need to undo it, lad, I've got a tow rope in the van.'

With the end of the rope secured to what looked like a solid place in the chassis of the coach, Tony eased the van forward but found the coach just wouldn't budge. Whacker's dad had said there was a brake shoe locked into place on one of the wheels, but Tony wondered if the wheel might slide along the floor, but it obviously wasn't going to. He didn't want to try too hard in case he damaged either the coach or the van – after all, he'd only borrowed it from his old works site.

Whacker, being the smallest one there, and now fairly familiar with the underside of the coach, offered to crawl underneath again to see if he could spot anything else that might be stopping it, but it was darker than he'd thought, and he had to come out for a torch. What he then found, in addition to the jammed brake shoe, was a wooden beam with one end lodged against the side wall and the other end between spokes of one of the wheels.

'Bit more of a problem than we thought,' he reported when he emerged. 'As well as the locked brake shoe, there's this beam that's jamming the back, left wheel, but I can't see how to shift it. The simplest would probably be to just saw it in two, but it's old timber, well seasoned, and may be under some tension. You'd have to know which side to cut so as not to get your saw trapped. If my dad was here, he'd probably have some ideas, but I'd not like to tackle it. And that timber could be valuable – and there seems to be a fair bit stacked against the back wall.'

'That's true,' joined in Mr W, 'the old master was always coming up with ideas of things he'd like to make – model windmills, rocking horses and stuff like that. And every idea had him going out to get the materials, only for him to soon lose interest. So yes, there might be timbers that are well worth having back there. I'd more or less forgotten about it.'

'Was he a cabinetmaker, then?' asked Whacker.

'Oh no. He'd been in engineering of some sort, company director, I believe, but the company was taken over, he was bought out and lived here in retirement. But he was always looking for something to do.'

'We're not sure when your dad is coming, are we, Whacker?' asked Tony. 'So I'll see if anybody at the yard has any ideas. I won't be long.' And off he went to the house to telephone some chaps he knew in the transport business he'd run.

Although Anna labelled and made notes about a few more pieces of furniture that Whacker selected, the excitement of the weekend had worn off, and all five of them slowed down waiting for Tony to give guidance on what should be done next.

CHAPTER 15

Back in the village, Eileen Bartlett was leading Slim along to her mobile library vehicle, an old single-decker bus donated by the local company. Unfortunately, it hadn't been repainted so, when it came in sight on its way to pick Eileen up, Slim immediately thought he was being sent home, and rounded on her, obviously still extremely upset.

'You promised! You all promised! You said – you said...' and he just stopped, his head dropped and he looked totally lost.

'Now, lad, don't fuss yourself so much. We said we'd not send you home alone and we'll not – this is my library bus and I'm hoping you'll come out on it with me today. You'll not see anybody you don't want to, and I'll take you back to the Red Lion to meet your pals this evening, if that's what you want. If not, you're welcome to stay with Graham, my husband, and me tonight – OK?'

'Oh, I'm sorry Mrs, er...?'

'Call me Eileen.'

'Right. Eileen – I'm sorry about how I'm behaving. I just don't know what's happening to me! I'm not like this! You ask Boots and Whacker – well perhaps not Whacker, he's a bit of a nut case at times. But they'll tell you I'm just not like this.' And he looked at Eileen so appealingly she almost gave him a big reassuring hug.

Trying not to sound concerned, Eileen asked if he could remember what the police doctor had said to him the day before.

'Well, apart from asking me what had happened – this bloke punching me in the face and shouting at me – he wanted to know if I'd lost consciousness at all, and I told him I didn't think I had. I guess he wanted to see if I was suffering from concussion. I think he decided I wasn't, but I'm not sure about that now. Why?'

He was so clear and confident about the doctor's examination that Eileen felt relieved and answered him honestly. 'I used to be a District Nurse, and I was wondering, too, if it could be the remains of a concussion that's affecting you. But I don't think so – I think you're more upset about what's happened with your pals, aren't you?'

'Well, it's not just them, it's the weekend, as well. I mean, it turned out nothing like we planned – we did no music – no playing, no writing – no exploring in the woods, no photos like we did when we were backpacking. It all revolved round that wretched Manor House and the people there. It's been a real waste of time and money. And now they've gone off and left me – no explanation – no apology – nothing. Yet they were more than happy for me to plan it and for my mum to arrange the rooms at the inn. I don't even know where they are now – do you?'

The arrival of the mobile library vehicle allowed Eileen to avoid telling him that she didn't really know, but had been told they were at the Manor. The driver had opened the door so she was able simply to usher Slim up the step and inside where he stopped, looked round and said, 'Wow, I'd never have believed you could get that many books into space like this!'

'Well, we have to, you know. People expect the same choice from us as they get in a town library – or perhaps a village library. And, of course, we can order items that we don't normally carry, just like any other branch. Anyway, let's get settled and we can be off to our first stop. OK Bill?'

Bill, obviously the driver, made sure they were using the seat belts then set off for their first stop in the village of Chaston. As the vehicle was a cast-off from the local bus company, it had definitely seen better days and was too noisy inside for any conversation, and this suited both Slim and Eileen. Slim's mind was really just a blank, while Eileen was beginning to wonder what she'd let herself, and possibly her husband, in for.

But, at the first stop, her initial fears were allayed as Slim immediately asked what he could do to help.

'You see the rack labelled Newly Returned Books? Well I'd like you to just move them into the shelf below, to make space for whatever people bring back next.'

'I could put them all back in their proper racks, if you like – it'll have to be done sooner or later, won't it?'

'It will, lad, but they serve a purpose staying up front here. You see, many folks are wary of being the first person to borrow a book, in case they don't like it or there's something perhaps offensive about it. They seem to think that if someone has borrowed it before them, that's a recommendation of it – even though they've no idea what the previous reader thought of it! It's daft really, but it's how some people are, so we like to leave a good few returned books out – and if the customers ignore the earlier returns, it means they're not seeming to be influenced by their neighbours!'

'Gosh! I never thought of librarians as having to be what – psychologists? – as well,' laughed Slim. And that laugh assured Eileen that he really was going to be OK and she'd have no problems with him being out on the library for the rest of the day.

'I think you need a bit of that in most walks of life, including your private life, especially if you're married!' she laughed. 'Anyway, there are some books you can put straight back where they belong, and that's the non-fiction. Have a look around and you'll get to know where the different categories are, but you'll probably only be handling biography and travel – they're the most popular.'

Before Slim could make further comments, Eileen had to turn to deal with the first of a group of three ladies bringing books back.

Feeling a bit lost, Slim picked up three of the books from the shelf she'd indicated, studied their titles, and carried them to the back of the bus looking for a place to put them. He was already used to the layout in his school library and the one in Bracknell town centre, but this space was so much smaller that the layout seemed quite different. He waited until Eileen had dealt with the batch of customers, and then asked her about it.

'Eileen, I've just taken those returned books back to their places, but they're all at the back – travel, biography, gardening and sport. Like you said, they seem to be the more popular categories, so I thought they'd be nearer the front to be handier.'

'Yes, that's how they do it in bigger libraries but, when you don't have so much space, if you had them near the front, all the customers that they attract would block the gangways and stop people getting to the other shelves, see?'

'Right! Now is that psychology or just basic planning?' and laughed.

'Well, it's a bit of both, really. We've found that folks going to the sections at the back often stop and look at something on the way there and end up exploring another topic. If you come across old Pete from the farm in Wayside, he reads up all about the military history of the places featured in the travel books – and he'll tell you about it at length, given chance!!'

'Thanks for the warning – is there anybody else I should avoid? Apart from the thug that mugged me, of course?'

'No, you'll be fine. Our customers are fairly set in their ways and don't often ask us to tell them where they'll find something. If they do, just refer them to me, OK?'

'That's a point, Eileen. I've never really thought about the different non-fiction categories before. How do you decide what books go where and what numbers to put on those little labels?'

'We don't have to do that, they come already coded, probably from the county library, but I'm not sure. We just put them in their proper places.'

'Is there a list of what the numbers on the labels mean? Have you got a copy so I can start to find my way around, please?'

'No, we haven't, I'm afraid. The best thing is just to get to know where the different topics are and look at the books in them and get the feel of the numbers. You'll soon see if anything's out of place, so just put it where it belongs. Same with the fiction, but they're all in alphabetical order of author's surname and they're all in one block, apart from crime and romance, but I expect you know that.'

'Yes, but what about a list of these numbers, please? There must be one somewhere, surely.'

'You mean the Dewey Decimal code.'

'You're joking,' he interrupted. 'Whoever heard of books – or anything, apart from eggs perhaps – being counted, and coded, in *dozens*!!'

'What are you on about, milad?'

'The code for the non-fiction books – duodecimal – counting in twelves instead of tens like in the decimal system.'

'It's not a "do…" – whatever you said – decimal code, it's the Dewey – d.e.w.e.y – decimal code. Invented by somebody Dewey, way back!'

'Sorry, sorry,' laughed Slim. 'Sorry Mr Dewey. I'll do what you told me, Eileen, and just find my way around.' And off he went to do just that.

Chapter 16

After what had become an uneventful afternoon, Eileen brought Slim back to the Red Lion to sort out with Jim what the plan was for Slim's immediate future. But the first people they met were Boots and Whacker heading off to their room to get ready for the evening meal.

'What are you doing here?' came from all three. This was followed by a bit of 'No, you first,' until Jim ushered them all into the Residents' Lounge so he could talk with Eileen.

'We thought you'd be home by now enjoying a bit of fuss from your mum,' started Boots. 'Did you miss the bus, or something?'

'No, I got on it all right and expected you two to jump on at the last minute – you know, just to have me on, like. But you didn't and I just threw a wobbly.'

This was the first the other two had heard of this and they just looked at Slim, open-mouthed.

'But you don't do things like that, Slim,' said Whacker. 'And we'd told you at breakfast that we're staying a few more days.'

'Right, I remember, but I reckoned you were just leg-pulling, you know? Anyhow, I just felt – I don't know – deserted, let down, I don't know, and I just went ape. Eileen reckons it was really the after-effects of that mugging I got yesterday. But I'm OK now,' and at last smiled.

'But where are you staying tonight?' asked Whacker. 'Can you still get home by bus in the evening?'

'Oh gosh, I'd completely not thought about that. My mum'll be worried sick when I'm not home on time. I've got to find out what's happening and give her a ring damn quick.'

As he headed for the door, it opened, and Jim came in closely followed by Eileen.

'Right, lads, let's get you up to date on what's been happening while you've been out and about. First off, Slim –

or Peter – we've been in touch with your mother and things have changed since your neighbour rang this morning.'

'My neighbour rang?'

'Sorry, yes, you were on your way out with Eileen here and, er, not really in a position to have dealt with it.'

'But what did she want? Is my mum OK?'

'Well, yes, she is, and what Mrs Harris had to say this morning has been overtaken by events and we've now got the latest picture from your mother. Knowing what happened, and that your pals are staying on for a few days...'

'A few days?' exclaimed Slim, looking accusingly at the other two, but mainly at Boots – Whacker could never have wangled a deal like that!

'No later than Thursday – or Friday at the latest,' replied Jim, hoping to calm things down a bit. 'She asked us to tell you what her situation is and what's been arranged, subject to your agreement, of course.'

'Oh. Well you'd best tell us what it is I'm supposed to agree to,' sounding rather annoyed. 'I'm off home on the bus as soon as poss, I assume.'

'Yes, of course that's one of the options, but it can't be today – the last bus that would make all the connections to Bracknell went at half past four. So, first off, Eileen and her husband Graham are offering you their son's bed for the night – or for a night or two longer if you want.'

'So, I can go home tomorrow, then?'

'Well, yes... but your mother is tied up all day tomorrow with meetings, she says. That's following her weekend trip and she'd be happy if you wanted to stay another day. In fact, she says she'd rather you stayed until she can come down and collect you. She says she's grateful for the help you've been given and wants to meet the people involved and thank them. All right so far?'

'Well, yes, but what about things like eating and having a bath and what do I do all day if Boots and Whacker are still tied up down at the Manor House, and stuff like that?'

Just then the Wilkinsons arrived and caught the end of the discussion. This allowed Mr W to intercede.

'For tomorrow, Slim, you and your pals can do whatever it was you came to do on your weekend here – Mr Philips has to go off to Salchester tomorrow, so there's nothing any of us can do at the Manor. So, we're all free to do what we want – well, we are every day, of course – we're only helping if we want to.'

'And,' Mrs W added, 'he asked us to tell you he'll pay for your meals this evening and tomorrow. He feels you've more than earned it.' As an aside to landlord Jim, she told him that Mr Philips had asked him to bill him for their meals at the Red Lion, after the lads' stay ended, if that was OK with him. And, of course, it was.

After this exchange, they all stood around not quite sure who should make the first move and what that move should be. Then Tina came in to tell Slim he should go to the office when he was ready to claim his pack and guitar. This prompted Eileen to suggest he pick it up now and take it to her house and settle in, if he was happy with that arrangement.

'Oh yes,' he replied, 'that would be great. But would you be offended if I came back here to have a meal with Boots and Whacker, and catch up and plan for tomorrow and that?'

'Actually, I'm glad you suggested it; I'd already prepared this evening's meal and there's only really enough for Graham and me, so if Jim can fit you all in that would be good. And I'll pay for your supper, so don't worry about that.'

'No, Eileen, you don't have to do that. Giving me a bed for the night is enough, and with Mr Philips feeding us over the weekend, I've still got some cash left. But thanks a lot for the offer.'

'Before you two start a fight,' interrupted Boots, 'can Whacker and I come with you just to see where Slim's going to be staying?'

'Of course you can, and you can meet my other half – though you may have seen him already when you came in on the bus the other day.'

So off they set and found that Eileen's house was almost within sight of the pub, the other side of the village green. Graham was already there and was introduced all round, but none of the lads could remember him from the bus ride into the village – and Graham kept quiet about them getting off the bus a couple of stops early and then walking in, though he did wonder what they'd been up to. Instead, he asked what he asked all new acquaintances – 'Do any of you play Crib?'

'Oh, Graham!' exclaimed his wife. 'Give the lads time to breathe! And how many folk of their age play Crib, anyway, these days?'

'I do – or I have done,' replied Slim, 'but it was a good few years ago and I can't really remember the details. My granddad taught me – mainly, I think to help with mental arithmetic, but I quite enjoyed it.'

Seeing his wife's expression, Graham replied, 'Right, lad, I leave it to you to say if you want to have a go at it – and I won't mind going over the rules and such to get you up to speed.'

While this was going on, Boots and Whacker had been looking on, open-mouthed.

'What on earth are you talking about, Slim?' asked Boots. 'I thought a crib was what you put babies in!'

'It's a card game where you take it in turns to play a card and try to make them add up to different totals – and at the same time try not to let the other player do just that. That's why it's good for mental arithmetic.'

'That's right, my lad,' replied Graham, 'and it doesn't half help if you're handling money like in a shop or on a bus, or working out how many bricks you need for a wall, and so on.'

'Don't start on that, love,' said Eileen, 'the lads are just here to see where we live so they can call on Slim if needed.

Now, it doesn't seem right to be calling you Slim – should I be using your proper name? If so, what is it?'

'Well it's Peter, but it's best to stick with Slim so you don't confuse my simple friends here!' and gave the best laugh they'd heard from him in days.

'Now then Slim, before a fight starts, let's show you your room and so-on then you can be off back for a meal at the Lion. If we're not quick about it, Graham will have your pals stuck into Crib for the evening.'

With that, Slim picked up his bag and followed her through to the stairs. As soon as they were out of sight, Graham got out a well-thumbed pack of cards and motioned Boots and Whacker to sit at the table so he could explain his favourite game. Obviously anticipating this move, Eileen was back in a flash and got him to put the cards away so she could lay the table for their evening meal. Seeing the lads looking a bit bemused, she explained, 'If I don't get him to make room for the food on the table I'm sure he'd never eat!' But it was said with a fond smile and no animosity.

Before the lads could respond, Slim reappeared after a (very) quick wash and they said their goodbyes and set off back to the Red Lion where they enjoyed a meal in the company, again, of Mr and Mrs Wilkinson.

'What are your plans for tomorrow then, lads, anything special?' asked Mr W.

'Nothing definite,' replied Slim, back in his role of spokesman for the band. 'That's how the weekend should have been, anyway.'

'Same with us as well, right, love?' asked Mr W. 'Sightseeing in Salchester.'

After the meal, the lads went off again to the bridge over the ford, gazed at the water and decided that tomorrow really would be a great day out – through the woods beyond the hay field, up the hill and a stretch out in the sun before a run-through of their latest numbers.

They got back to the Red Lion just before closing time and again, (was it really by accident?) Whacker found Tina ready for a late stroll around the village green. And again she accepted his offer to escort her and this time he managed to touch, and then tentatively hold, her hand – and she didn't resist!

Chapter 17

The fine weather was continuing and the visitors staying at the Red Lion in Charlford were all in optimistic mood as they enjoyed their breakfasts. The Wilkinsons announced that they'd be sightseeing in Salchester, while Boots and Whacker assumed they'd be off into the countryside once Slim arrived from Eileen and Graham's. So they all moved off out of the dining room to prepare for the day.

Tina had heard their plans and suggested to her dad that they should offer the lads a packed lunch for their day in the countryside – the Wilkinsons would have ample choice of eateries in Salchester. He agreed, realising it was partly her liking of one of the lads that had prompted the suggestion; but he didn't mind, as the lads would soon be off and out of her life, allowing her to concentrate on her work and get ready to return to school.

The Wilkinsons were the first to leave, catching the bus driven by Graham, who, having heard a bit about them from Slim, greeted them like long-lost friends and made sure they knew the times of the buses back from the city. This auspicious start convinced them that they'd have to see about extending their stay in the area, so would look around for a room in the city in case the Red Lion couldn't let them stay on.

As for the lads, Slim arrived at the Red Lion full of energy after a good night's sleep and a hearty breakfast, guitar slung on his back and ready to head out into the countryside. While the others were pleased to see him back in good spirits, Whacker sensed that this was Slim in full management mode and hoped the day wouldn't be too serious.

On handing over their packed lunches, including one for Slim, Tina reminded Boots, 'Don't forget the meat voucher you won in the Tell-a-Tale event.'

'Oh, I'd completely forgotten about it. What can I do with it? Would your dad like to have it?' he asked.

'It's kind of you, but we're not allowed to use it – the butcher that donates it would assume we'd just kept it and not offered it as a prize.'

'I'm sure our parents wouldn't want to be carrying meat all the way home to Bracknell,' said Boots, 'so how would it be if I gave it to Slim for him to give to Eileen as thanks for having him?'

'That would be fine, and a lovely gesture that I'm sure she'd appreciate. I'll go and tell Dad in the hope that he'll remember to deal with it when you come back this evening.'

With that, they said their 'cheerios' and the lads set off once more down the road to the ford where they again stood watching the waters gently flowing along towards Charlbury, the spiritual home of their heroes, The Mystic Wizards.

'We really ought to go there one day, you know,' said Whacker – a suggestion he'd put forward many times before. 'If we didn't take our instruments and just went as regular visitors or tourists, or whatever you'd call us, we could just soak up the atmosphere, visualise the songs, and perhaps come away more inspired.'

'OK,' said Slim, 'why not do it now? We don't really know when we can get back here again, do we? It's only four or five miles, we can get there in time to have our lunches in the Ambient Field, get a drink in the pub where they stayed, and get back in time for dinner here, and no rush. How about it?'

'You sure we'd be able to find the Ambient Field, Slim?' asked Boots. 'I mean, we've never seen it on a map, have we?'

'One way to find out, O ye of little faith!! All in favour?'

No-one replied – they'd already turned as one to go back and leave their guitars in their room at the Red Lion and transfer their packed lunch into Boots' backpack. It was only then that they realised they weren't sure if there was a footpath all the way between the villages. Jim and Tina, watching all their comings and goings, assured them that there was a path there – a continuation of the path that went past Eileen's cottage. So off they went.

There was no urgency to their journey and they stopped occasionally to watch a bird or examine a plant, but all the time they talked about the experiences the weekend had brought – until it came to Slim's turn.

'Well, I'd rather not have been mugged, but at least it happened in time for me to realise, before it's too late, how I feel about physical violence. I know now that police work isn't for me.'

That was a bombshell that the others had not expected and they stopped, glanced at each other, then stared at Slim before they let out a simultaneous, 'YOU WHAT?'

Boots was first to muster and express a coherent thought. 'But you've ALWAYS been going to join the police, Slim. It's what you are – a policeman in waiting.'

'Yeah, well things can change. And, as I said, I changed my mind before it was too late.'

'But what are you going to do?' asked Boots. 'You're made for a job where you sort things out and organise things and people – what other job gives you that? You've got to have some ideas ready for when you have to choose your subjects and so on when we start back at school.'

'Don't get in a fret, mate. I got a great idea working in the mobile library yesterday.'

'Don't tell us you're going to be a librarian, Slim! OK, it's an important job, but there'd be no *people* for you to organise and such,' was Whacker's contribution.

'No, course not. It was a book I found'

'Good place to find a book,' jumped in Whacker, earning a dig in the ribs from Boots.

'Come on, Slim, spit it out – tell us all about it, you know you want to,' from Boots.

'Well, it was a careers book first that mentioned the legal profession, then quite near to it was one that was about just that – jobs in the legal profession! I took it as an omen.'

'Hope you don't mean that "literally"!! – Joke – took a book – literally!!' Whacker couldn't resist.

'Give over, Whacker. Give him a chance or we'll be here all day!'

'Well,' continued Slim, 'that's more or less it. The book makes it look like I can get into the legal system, but be a step or two away from the physical harm bits. Still dealing with baddies and making sure they get their just desserts, but in a cleaner, tidier way. So, there you have it, I've decided I should aim for the lawyer part of the system.'

'Wow, Slim! I don't know what to say. Can you just decide like that? I mean, don't you have to go to special law schools or something like you read about in American crime novels?'

'According to what I understand from this book, you probably need a degree, but it doesn't always have to be a law degree. Not sure of the details but it seems like law companies need people that specialise in other things like finance and art and whatever they do the legal stuff for.' And then his ideas sort of petered out.

'I think you really need to get hold of that book again and make sure you've got it right before you start talking about it at school,' said Boots, hoping that that ended the subject.

'That's the plan for tomorrow,' replied Slim, who could tell he'd certainly not convinced the other two about the idea. 'I'm going on the mobile library again and I'll ask Eileen if I can borrow that book, or if she can check if there's a copy in the library back home.'

'Good idea – oh no, bad idea,' was Whacker's response as they turned a corner and found their path blocked by a fence bordering a field. There was a proper footpath sign and a stile to get over the fence, but the field was occupied by a large group of young cattle. Being townies at heart, none of them was happy about the idea of trying to go through the field.

'I guess Charlbury will have to wait for another day,' was Boots' view. 'I know we said this could be our last weekend here, but we could always do just a day run there by bus. OK?'

'Oh, come on,' argued Slim, 'there's got to be a way through or round this.'

But, without forcing a way through brambles that grew up to the fence, a fairly thorough check couldn't find a route to bypass the cattle. So eventually they all agreed with Boots and set off back to Charlford and go for the walk they'd originally planned, starting out over the ford and through the hay field.

If the boys had only known it, their attempt to reach Charlbury had been blocked at the very edge of what their heroes, the Mystic Wizards, had called The Ambient Field – the area that had inspired some of their best-loved music. Would that prove to be an omen for the future of The Acolytes?

Meanwhile, the Wilkinsons were enjoying a leisurely stroll through the once-familiar streets of Salchester, and gradually realising they had not really known the city all that well. Their visits had mainly been on errands for the family at Charlford Manor, so their own leisure time had been too precious to spend in the same place and they'd taken trips to Oxford or Winchester, and sometimes to London.

Now they wanted to see the place as if they were tourists on their first visit, so they headed for the cathedral. They declined the offer of the services of the guides and just wandered around, soaking up the beauty and colour of the stained glass windows and gazing in amazement at the delicacy of the stone carvings, all created so long ago by craftsmen using only the simplest of tools.

After a while, their feet and aching necks told them it was time for a coffee break, so they headed out looking for somewhere familiar to take their break. They found that one or two of the premises had changed their use, some to cater for an increased tourist trade, while one that once had been a quality gents' outfitters, now stocked prams and babywear – a change that saddened them. But eventually they found the bakery that they both remembered and went in, hoping that it still had a teashop and that their memories wouldn't be spoiled by any changed reality.

'Good morning, do you still serve tea and cakes?' asked Mrs W of the lady behind the counter.

'Of course we do, Mrs Jenkins – er, it *is* Mrs Jenkins, isn't it? Forgive me if I'm wrong, but you so remind me of a Mrs Jenkins who was a regular customer a few years ago.' And she blushed very slightly in case she'd caused offence.

'Well, you're right, it is me, but no longer Mrs Jenkins, I'm a Wilkinson now. This is my husband, Harry, who did come in once or twice, dare I say "in the old days", but never with me. We were both at Charlford Manor, but didn't marry until after we'd left – you may have heard something of that event, perhaps,' she replied with a wry smile to show she was not offended.

'Well, yes, the rumour mill was working as you'd expect but, as you might guess, we were never sure what to believe – and when I say "we", I mean the locals, mainly trade folk, you know, the ones that had dealings with the Manor. We heard there'd been a rumpus – though not as interesting as when old Mr Hawkins left the place – and it soon settled down.'

'As far as we were concerned,' Mr W joined in, 'the sooner we were away the better. Mary, here, was well away from that husband of hers, and I'm lucky that she chose to stick with me, eh, love?'

'Give over, Harry, you're making me blush, and you're embarrassing – I'm sorry, but I don't even know your name. I know it's Hilda's Bakery and Tea Shop, but are you Hilda? We always assumed you were.'

'No, Hilda was my mother-in-law. I'm Joan Matthews, and pleased to meet you again.'

And, somewhat late in the proceedings, they all shook hands. Then the Wilkinsons were shown to a table in the window in the upstairs tearoom and their order of tea and cakes served – 'compliments of the house'.

After a while, Joan rejoined them and they chatted about the town, how some things had changed and others were still apparently the same. At last the conversation got around to what the Wilkinsons were doing now.

'Have you come back to Charlford to live, to work, or just to visit? And what is happening at the Manor? And how is Tony Philips?'

Joan Matthews managed to rattle off this barrage of questions almost without pause for breath, then abruptly stopped, blushed and explained that she needed to know on behalf of the trades people in the town. (The gossip machine, thought both Mr and Mrs W.)

'We are all a bit concerned about Tony; he is really well-liked, and folks wonder if he'd jumped into buying Charlford Manor without giving it enough thought. People think it was probably on the rebound of having his wife walking out on him.'

These questions put the Wilkinsons in a bit of a spot as they quite liked Tony and felt a sense of loyalty towards him. As usual, it was Mrs W who gave their reply, doing her best to avoid disclosing anything she felt was confidential.

'Oh, he's doing just fine there. It seems the place needed a fair amount of updating and that's more or less done now. We gave him a hand with the running of things for his daughter's birthday last weekend and we'll perhaps help him in one or two staffing matters before deciding on our next move.' That was all the answer she wanted to give concerning the Manor, so moved on to their own situation.

'We've actually retired now and came here as a first stop on a bit of a tour of places we've worked – hoping we'll get an idea of where we'd like to settle. When you're in service you have no choice about where you live, unless you dislike a location strongly enough to leave the position – and that never happened to us. We've only moved on under our own steam, as it were, when the families moved abroad or changed their lifestyle.'

'So, would you settle here if Tony offered you positions working for him?' asked the persistent Joan Matthews.

'I don't think that's likely to happen, but we're happy to give any advice or opinions if asked,' was as non-committal as Mrs W could get.

'I'm sorry if it sounded too much like prying,' Joan persisted, 'but the reason I asked is that, if you were to be in the area, I think you could be in demand to advise employers, and perhaps help to train staff for domestic service. How does that appeal?'

This was so totally unexpected that the Wilkinsons could only look at each other open-mouthed. But this time it was Mr W who was first ready to reply.

'If somebody has been repeating bits of conversations heard at the Manor over the weekend, then they're making too much of a casual remark or two. Yes, it was suggested that we might help Mr Philips to decide what staff he might need, and then perhaps help him select the best applicant, and even offer advice on job descriptions – to use a modern term. But that was the extent of it. Our plans are still to tour around a bit and then decide where we want to settle.'

'Right,' Joan replied, 'but that doesn't seem to be saying no to the idea of providing – shall we say – a consulting service, if you choose to settle within reach of the city, does it?'

'Look, Joan,' joined in Mrs W, 'you seem to have a very clear idea of what service you think we can provide, so do you also have an idea of the customers?'

'Alright, it looks like it's time for cards on the table. A good friend of my daughter's runs a staffing agency and finds it difficult to find and supply trained or experienced domestic staff. And it's becoming a real problem. There are plenty of people who want the work and who think that the way they do things at home is good enough. I feel that a little of the support that you could give would go a long way. What do you think?'

'Don't look at me,' said Mr W, 'Mary is the more experienced one, but neither of us is qualified to teach and, really, we do need a break.'

Sensing that the idea hadn't been totally dismissed, Joan Matthews kept quiet except to call for one of her staff to bring them fresh drinks. The waitress who brought the drinks told Mrs Matthews she was needed in the bakery downstairs, so the Wilkinsons took the opportunity to quickly finish their drinks and leave the premises, pleased to get away from any further questions.

'What now?' asked Mr W, as they came out into the warm summer sunshine. 'I mean now, as in today, not as in the rest of our lives.'

'I don't know – she really unsettled me with all those questions *and* those hints that Mr Philips may be having problems. She tried to sound like a friend, but I bet she just wanted gossip to take back to her trades cronies.' A pause, then she continued, 'But I could be reading it all wrong. I just wanted today to be a nice touristy day and all those questions were spoiling the mood. Come on, let's forget her and go and sit in the park by the river – given time, I think I'll have room for an ice cream!' So that's what happened.

CHAPTER 18

The Wilkinsons were not really surprised, when they came into the dining room next morning, to find Boots and Whacker well into their breakfasts.

'Big day then, lads?' enquired Mr W, rather unnecessarily.

'Oh, leave them alone,' responded Mrs W. 'I'm sure you're as keen as they are to see what the coach looks like when they get it out of its – whatever you call it – and see if it still works alright.'

'That's right,' said Whacker, 'and to see what my dad makes of the items I've marked for him to have a look at.'

'Why's that important?' Mr W asked.

'Well, mainly it's a chance to see how my ideas compare with his but, between you and me, I'm hoping it gets him thinking I'm good enough for an apprenticeship.'

'You're sure you're not just looking for an excuse not to go back to school, are you?' asked Mrs W, looking quite concerned.

'Oh no. I'd carry on at school, or Tech College, but also be getting practical training as a cabinetmaker; and that's what I really want to do. So, I just hope Dad thinks I'm good enough. Anyway, find out soon. We're off – if you'll excuse us.' And he would have been off out of the door if Tina hadn't appeared just then bringing toast and coffee to a nearby table.

'Does that mean you want to be off today?' she asked, rather quietly, and slightly blushed.

'Course not, no – er, no,' stammered Whacker. 'Not at all. It's just that Dad's decision is important – but he doesn't know it yet. Anyway, we're staying as long as we can. And I DO want to see you again this evening, if that's alright?'

Before Tina could reply, the lads had disappeared, Whacker blushing like mad, up to their room to get ready for the day.

'Don't worry, love,' interceded Mrs W, 'he's an honest lad and he won't go off without spending as much time with you as he can, you mark my words. Now, if you're free, hubby and I are ready for our toast and coffee, please.' And things returned to normal.

Slim turned up at the door of the Red Lion just as Boots and Whacker were about to set off. 'Are you going to need me today?' he asked no-one in particular. 'Only, if not, Eileen says she can use some help on the mobile library, and she can get me back here when my mum turns up.'

'Well, we're not really sure what's happening as yet,' answered Boots. 'It depends a bit on Whacker's dad and if they can move the coach. I reckon if you've got a job lined up, you'd best go and do it – I'm sure we'll be OK. Oh, and say hello to your mum for us, OK?'

'Great, thanks,' was all they got from Slim as he hurried off to return to his new interest.

By this time the Wilkinsons were also ready to go, so they set off together yet again, each of them privately enjoying being part of the group, gaining personal support and encouragement, and enjoying the company of a different generation and new audiences for their comments and ideas. And deep down, each of them realised how much they would miss it when the time came to move on.

Arriving at the Manor, they headed straight for the stable yard, attracted by calls of 'Forward a bit, Bill', then 'Steady', then 'No, sorry, a bit more to the left' and finally 'OK, that should do it.' This final comment came as they turned into the yard and saw a solid-looking truck backed up towards the open coach house doors. The driver – obviously the 'Bill' in the sequence – had jumped down from the cab and was walking to the back of the vehicle to check his partner's opinions.

When he saw them, he stopped and called out, 'Sorry, but you can't come in here, it's private land and on top of that this manoeuvre might be a bit tricky. If you're looking for Mr Philips, he'll be here in a minute, but you'd best stay outside the gates.'

With that, he carried on to the rear of the truck and got into conversation with his partner, assuming the group would do as he asked – and, of course, they would have done if they'd had no connection with the place. But they were all a bit put out and didn't quite know how to deal with the situation until Whacker, apparently driven by the strongest incentive, called out, 'Mr Philips is expecting us so, when you see him, please tell him the Wilkinsons and the Acolytes are here – and we're waiting to start work!'

Before this conversation could develop, Tony and Anna arrived and invited the group into the yard. Tony made vague introductions – 'chaps from the garage' and 'friends helping with the house' – then took the group to a spot near the old laundry building where they could watch the work being done in the entrance to the coach house.

'What's happened so far,' he said, 'is that the coach's shaft – not sure if that's the right word for the beam the horses are attached to – that's been lowered, as you can see, and they've got it level with the back of the truck ready to tow the coach out, but the problem is working out how to secure it to the truck's tow hook.'

'Couldn't they just use a rope to pull it out?' asked Boots.

'That's what I thought at first but, having spoken to Whacker's dad, we realised we don't know what state the wheels and axles will be in. So the lads from the garage came up with the idea of using dollies. That means we don't have to try to use the wheels, but you know what dollies can be like – liable to run all over the place, depending on how level the land is.'

This was met with a stunned silence, eventually broken by Whacker. 'I don't know about the rest of us, Tony, but I haven't got a clue what you're talking about! What's "dollies"? I know what trolley dollies are in aircraft, but just plain "dollies"?'

'Sorry. If you'd been in the house when the furniture movers were working you'd have seen one then – it's a small square board with a caster wheel at each corner. You tilt up a piece of heavy furniture, like a wardrobe or a filing cabinet, roll the dolly under it, lower the piece onto it then it's easier to move it around.' Seeing the looks of general understanding he ploughed on. 'What they're using here is a tougher version of that, based on a shopping trolley. We got a contract a few months ago to clear out some old trolleys when Bennett's supermarket was upgrading their "fleet" and we made ourselves a few dollies from them, and they've been really useful.'

'So that's why you need to use the coach's shaft instead of a rope to pull it out,' said Mr W, 'it could roll anywhere with just casters under it. Very clever.'

'But how do you get it onto these dolly things?' Boots wanted to know.

'Oh, that should be easy. We use standard jacks from the garage, but we do have to be careful finding places under the coach that can take the pressure and not collapse. A basic problem is that we don't really know how heavy the coach is – so it's all a bit delicate. There's a chance something might break and send wood splinters flying around. That's why we need to keep you all out of the way, as far as we think it will be safe.'

'What about the beam of wood I found jammed between the spokes of one of the back wheels?' asked Whacker. 'That looked like it would stop any movement in any direction.'

'That was one of the first things they sorted,' replied Tony with a chuckle. 'Young Charlie went under there with his big hammer and gave it what he calls "a technical tap" – in other words, a hefty clout. Anyway, it did the trick and no apparent harm done, but we'll see better when we get the vehicle out. He had a look at the brake shoe that's jammed against the back wheel, but couldn't see where the problem lay, so again we'll have a better look when it's outside.'

While this chat had been going on, the wheels at the front of the coach had been jacked up and Charlie was getting down to lie on his back on what looked like a wide plank of wood. Then, with a push of his feet, he shot along the ground and disappeared under the coach – a process that was met with a gasp from the younger onlookers.

'What on earth was that?' asked Slim.

'It's called a creeper,' explained Mr W. 'Again, it's just a board with small wheels, like a dolly, but very useful – and not as dangerous as a skateboard!' he ended with a chuckle.

'Round here, Mr Wilkinson, it's called a crawler – but it does the same job. Yet if you used the same names to describe a person, it's not so pleasant. Ah, well, that's the English language for you. Anyway, we should see some action soon.'

Bill, the other garage man, sent a couple of the dollies rolling along the ground to follow his mate, Charlie, under the coach toward the back wheels.

'They've not put any dollies under the front wheels yet,' observed Boots.

'No, they first want to get it sorted out at the back where it's less easy to operate – then they can control things from the front of the coach where they can make quick adjustments if things start to go wrong.'

'What sort of things do you think might go wrong?' asked Whacker, privately glad that his dad wasn't around if things were to go wrong.

'Nothing should, lad, so don't worry, but we don't really know much at all about the coach – mainly we don't know how heavy it is and if the wheels are still in good shape or not. Once we start to tow it out we'll be a lot happier. For now, the chaps are putting chocks under the truck's wheels, to help stabilise it in case the coach runs out a bit sharpish and gives it a push, but it should all be fine.'

By this time the back wheels of the coach were up on dollies and strapped to them so they couldn't roll off, and Charlie had emerged from under the coach ready to do the same to the front ones.

'Making good progress, I see,' said Whacker's dad, announcing his arrival and shaking hands with Tony. 'And I brought along some extra effort if needed,' and he indicated Slim who'd followed him in.

'What happened to you, Slim?' asked Boots. 'Did the library go without you?'

'Or have you finished reading all the books?' laughed Whacker.

'Ha-ha, Whacker! No, it wouldn't start, and they'd no idea how soon it could be fixed, OK?'

'Good to see you, lad. Don't mind these two, you're very welcome,' said Tony, then turned his attention back to Whacker's dad.

'Did you try turning the wheels while they're jacked up, Tony, before fixing them to the dollies? If they're OK it would save fitting them to the dollies and then having to jack them up again to get them off – worth a try I reckon, and you only need to see if they spin freely.'

'If they spin freely with no weight on, do you think it means they'll be OK taking their full load? I didn't really want to risk it,' replied Tony.

'Should be OK, assuming the carriage is empty right now, but you'd need to check with an expert before taking any load on board, and you'd need that check for the whole structure anyway.'

'You're right, I reckon it's worth at least trying to give them a spin. I'll have a word with the lads.' And off Tony went to do just that. After some discussion, it was clear to the onlookers that the chaps from the garage didn't want the responsibility of trying to turn the wheels in case there was a problem, and Tony came back to speak to Whacker's dad.

'Can you come over and do this with me, or at least tell me how much pressure I can put on the wheels if they don't turn straight away?' Seeing Ted's hesitation, he quickly added – 'I take full responsibility and, really, when I think about it, even if the carriage breaks into small bits, I've lost nothing as long as nobody gets hurt.'

'You know I'm no expert, at least on carriages, but I'm happy to give you a hand.'

So, they returned to the front wheel that Tony had already looked at, and Ted offered to try turning it. As he expected, it just wouldn't move until he pressed much harder on the outer end of one of the spokes; this resulted in a small cracking sound before the wheel started to turn. At that, Ted told Tony that they should leave it as it really would need lubricating, and that further turning might just damage the hub.

The garage chaps had been watching and acted on Tony's signal to carry on with fixing the front wheels to the dollies, ready to tow the carriage out. Soon, Bill was in the truck with the engine running, while Charlie checked that each wheel was secured to its dolly. When the last one was clear, the truck was inched forward and the coach followed it meekly, and rather ignominiously, on it's set of dollies, and was greeted with a cheer and applause from the audience.

'I'm afraid the truck can't stay here much longer,' said Tony, 'so we'd better check that we can move the carriage by hand before they leave – any idea, lads?' he called to them.

'We'll unlash it from the tow bar and see what happens, if you like,' replied Bill, and got on with it without waiting for a reply. Charlie took the strain in case the carriage moved on its own – but it didn't, demonstrating that the surface in that part of the stable yard was as level as they'd thought. 'It's clear, Charlie, so hold it there, then we'll see if we can push it back towards the coach house.'

It wasn't easy, but the two young men soon had it rolling steadily, and then stopped it quite easily. 'There you are, Mr Philips, let's see how many of you it takes to do the same. Bear in mind the ground is nice and dry at the moment so you wouldn't want to try this after rain if the surface was still wet.'

'Oh dear,' said Tony, 'I hadn't thought about that. My friends here are just visiting and I can't ask them to get involved in something like that. Tell you what, if we could leave it somewhere out here and be sure it won't roll around, could you come back later this afternoon, say, and push it back into the coach house for me? We need it out here in the yard while we have a good look at it and see what's stored behind it.'

'No problem, Mr P, we can chock up all the dollies to stop them rolling and then come back about four, if that's OK?'

'Yes, that's great, thanks.'

To stop the dollies rolling, they put some rope on the ground around each set of wheels, and that seemed to do the job, yet would easily be taken away when the carriage was to be moved. With a couple of final calls of 'Take care, and give us a bell if you have any problems', Charlie and Bill drove off back to the garage in Salchester.

For a couple of moments nobody moved, then Tony stepped forward towards the coach and said, 'Right, folks, let's see just what I've inherited. Has it been worth the wait and the trouble to move it or not? What do you think?' he asked, turning to Whacker's dad.

'As I just said, I'm no expert, but it looks fine and it certainly moved well. Just hope the doors aren't locked and there's a step somewhere to help us climb in. But, Tony,' he continued, putting his hand on Tony's arm to get his attention, 'I really need to have a word as soon as you can get clear for a minute.'

'That sounds serious, so let's just get the carriage open and the youngsters can explore it and have a play at being stage coach drivers, OK?'

The coach door wasn't locked and they soon let down the set of steps to help them climb in. But before anyone could do that, a couple of small packages slid out and landed at Tony's feet.

'What the…?' he exclaimed, then bent and picked them up to reveal that they had been sent by post, addressed to the wife of the previous owner, were fairly heavy for their size and hadn't been opened. He passed them to Anna, and the others all gathered round her to have a look. Tony moved closer to the coach to have a proper look inside and saw that there were more such packages strewn across the seats and on the floor. While some had plain wrappings, most carried the logo and name of a book club he'd never heard of.

'Right folks,' he said, turning back to the others, 'this is a puzzle solved.'

'How come, Dad?' asked Anna. 'Surely it's as much as a mystery as the coach itself.'

'Well it would be, but when I asked my solicitor about what to do with the coach he checked with the family's solicitor. He was told that the family were so scattered around the world that it had been difficult to pin down on who was to have what. But they all finally agreed that if we found anything else we should just accept it and do as we chose with it. BUT they would be interested to know if we found any books that had come from a book club – and this looks like them.'

'And they want them, Dad, is that it?'

'No, they just asked to be informed if any turn up anywhere. It seems that in the late owner's bank account they found this standing order for books, but couldn't see any books anywhere that it might have bought. They cancelled the payment order, of course, but wondered if this book club was actually a fraud – looks like it wasn't. But the solicitors said they certainly didn't want the problem of seeing if any family members wanted them, and it seems that the family agreed. Anyway, I'll give my solicitor a ring so he can pass the word along – and I suppose I'd better wait till they confirm their lack of interest before I do anything with them.'

'Job for Super Librarian Slim, by the look of it,' laughed Whacker, and they all joined in, including Slim.

'What you can do, lads,' continued Tony, 'is move the parcels into the coach house next door and stack them up until I know what I can do with them, then we can have a proper look at the coach. Now, Ted, let's go up to the house and grab a coffee while you tell me what it is you want to talk about.' So off they went, with Ted refusing to start his piece until they were settled in the dining room with coffees that Mrs W had produced.

'Right, Tony,' Ted started, somewhat hesitantly, 'you might think I've got a nerve to ask, but are you still not decided on how you're going to use these houses and which one you want to live in?'

'No, feel free to ask. Situation's not changed in that department – I'm still open to ideas and suggestions, so fire away.'

'Well, like I said last weekend, I'd love to be able to work here, so much more pleasant than the unit I've got in the industrial estate back home, and I've got contacts and customers around Oxford and even a couple this side. So my wife and I talked things over when we got home, in fact we seem to have talked of nothing but, since we got in the car to go home. Anyway, the upshot is that we wondered if we could rent the small house from you as well as renting a workshop – a coach house or perhaps even two. There,' he ended and looked relieved at having got it off his chest.

'Right. Let's think about it. First off, would you want a short-term rent while you see how it works out?'

'Well we did wonder if that might be an option, but it would make more sense if we thought of it as long-term, or perhaps even permanent, mainly from my business point of view. You see, there'd be all my workshop kit and materials to move, and then there's Whacker's education to sort out. In fact, that last point means it would be nice, but not critical I think, to get decisions sooner rather than later.'

'OK. But I didn't expect to need to make this sort of decision as soon as this, so perhaps this is just the kick I needed to get started. Let me make a couple of phone calls while you have a proper look at the place. I guess you and your wife really need that second look round to help decide if this is what you really want – Anna could show you round the cottage, if you like. But what about Whacker? If he's been in on the discussion he's certainly kept it under his hat!'

'That's the other thing – we've not mentioned it to him and he'd have to move schools, but I think I can offer something that may tip the balance. I'll go see him and Alison while you make your calls and, perhaps, reach your decision.'

'I don't know how long my queries will take, but we'll need a spot of lunch at some time, so I'll book us some tables up at the Red Lion for about half twelve, how's that? Then if either side has anything to say, we can do it then and the other side will know what to do next – OK?'

'Sounds just about right, thanks.'

'Oh, and if you see Boots or Slim, could you ask one of them to bring a couple of those parcels of books up here? I want to see what they're like and if they'd fit into the library shelving.'

'Will do.'

All the discussions about possibly moving to Charlford had pushed the prospect of studying the newly-found carriage to the back of Ted's mind, but the sight of it standing clear of the coach house got him excited again. On its first appearance, the jumble of parcels spilling from the seats onto the floor had made it look a bit scruffy and had spoiled the glamour of it for him. But now, with only a couple of parcels still inside, it looked ready to have a pair of horses harnessed and be off on a journey! And his wife, Alison, who was standing there, looked as if she might share the vision. He was brought to earth as the lads and Anna emerged from the coach house having taken in the last of the parcels of books.

'Doesn't she look great?' he managed. 'Almost ready for the road, I'd say – after a bit of a spruce up, of course.'

'Count me out for that,' said Anna, 'and those books are heavier than I thought – and dustier!'

'Actually, Anna, your dad has a different job in mind for you. He'd like you to show my wife around the cottage if that's OK. And he also asked if Boots or Slim could take a couple of these parcels of books up to the house for him to have a look at. As for me, I'd like Whacker to have a close look at the carriage with me.' There was no dissent from that and the others set off towards their different destinations on their allotted tasks.

'What's the programme then, Dad? Don't forget you're going to look at those pieces of furniture as well as the coach.'

'No, I've not forgotten, but the job here is simply to check what state the coach is in – get an idea if it's worth him keeping it or not. So, you climb inside and look to see if there are any holes or cracks or gaps at any of the joints, and so on. You'll soon see any if the sun shines through. I'm going to check round the outside to see how solid it looks and what the surfaces look like. Really, it should all be OK. It's been inside in what seems to be a dry atmosphere, but you never can tell.'

'How do I mark any gaps, Dad?'

'Hang on a minute, I've got a piece of chalk here – that should do it. But write them down as well so we can look at it afterwards. Oh, and don't worry about the seats just yet – we'll only have them looked at if Tony decides the coach is worth doing up.'

So they got on with it and were soon absorbed in their separate tasks. Whacker had never sat in a horse-drawn carriage before and was surprised at how small it seemed, with not much legroom between the seats, and there wasn't really enough height for him to stand comfortably. But this latter fact made it easier for him to find and mark the few holes and cracks he found in the roof. Checking the sides was more difficult as he had the light from outside in his eyes, even on the shade side of the coach. He was about to step out of the coach, thinking he'd done a good job, when he felt a small part of the floor sag a bit under his foot. He finally completed the check of the inside by lifting the carpet and noting quite a soft spot of flooring just inside the door – obviously the place where everybody put their foot and full weight as they stepped into, as well as out of, the coach. And he felt quite pleased with that discovery and his reasoning.

Finding his dad at the rear of the coach, they checked each other's list of things needing attention and agreed it looked like the coach was well worth repairing, so they then moved inside to assess the stack of timbers that had been stored behind the coach. It all seemed fairly ordinary stuff that might be bought for domestic DIY tasks; then they got to the very back and discovered some beautiful veneers, planks and posts. Ted was of the opinion that this was material left over from the days when the coach was built, and thus well worth keeping.

'Right, lad, let's tidy this up so there's room for the coach to be brought back in, then we can go up to the house and see what you made of the pieces of furniture you looked at.'

They had barely finished putting things straight when they heard a very loud and angry-sounding voice, followed by an expression of complete surprise, followed by more angry shouting. It seemed to be coming from the next-door coach house so they both ran out there and were just in time to see Mr Wilkinson snarling at a shocked-looking Slim, 'If you know what's good for you you'll stop poking your nose where it doesn't belong and you'll keep your damned mouth shut about this!'

But, as soon as Ted and Whacker appeared, Mr W stopped snarling and took on his usual genial appearance, albeit still flushed from his anger.

'Everything all right here?' asked Ted, even though it obviously wasn't.

'Yes, no problems,' replied Mr W. 'I was just picking up a small retirement gift I'd got for the wife – I'd hidden it back here a couple of days ago. When you're living in a hotel room like we are, there's nowhere you can be sure she won't find it before the day. Anyway, it seems young Slim here got the idea I was stealing it and, I suppose, was just looking out for what he thought could be Mr Philips' possessions. That's all it was.'

'The way you reacted, I thought I was right, too!' exclaimed Slim, still looking somewhat shaken by Mr W's response to his approach.

'Well, you see, that was something I'd always wanted the chance to do. You won't have come across that old film star baddy, Eddie something, but that was sort of his catchphrase they seemed to work into all his films – "If you know what's good for you" and so on. So, when you startled me, it just came out – more or less subconsciously. Sorry if I alarmed you, lad, but I'd really appreciate it if you could all keep quiet about this – the gift, I mean. I want it to be a real surprise for Mrs W.'

'Seems no harm's done,' replied Ted, 'so let's get up to the house, Whacker. You coming too, Slim? See you later, perhaps at lunch time in the Red Lion, Mr Wilkinson.'

Getting nods all round they all set off. Ted got a fairly firm grip on Slim's arm to keep him between himself and Whacker, then launched into a fairly loud chat about the great state of the coach. When he felt sure Mr W was off on the way up to the village he pulled the lads to a stop and asked, 'Now then, Slim. What really happened back there? Was he really as angry as he sounded and, if so, had you done anything to cause it – I need you to tell me the truth here.'

'Honest, Mr Bailey, he looked really suspicious. I'd just gone in to pick up a couple of those parcels of books when I saw him. He turned round from the back corner and he'd got this small box in his hands. It looked to me very much like one that my gran had and she called it her jewellery box. It'd got little compartments inside for rings and brooches and things, and it had got a soft cloth finish to it, inside and outside. But Mr W's was all covered in cement dust and I'm sure he'd got it out of a hole I saw in the wall when he moved away. That's not something he'd hidden a few days ago, if you ask me. Anyway, you couldn't get to that back wall until today because of all the stuff stored against it. I reckon it's fishy.'

'But did you say or do anything that might have startled him?'

'No, I don't think so. I just walked in as he was turning away from the back wall – and he just started in at me, like you heard. I'm sure something's not right there.'

'OK, but if you're right, best not to confront him or do anything to trigger another outburst.' Pause for thought, then, 'Look, Slim, I think it best if I have a quiet word with Mr Philips – see if anything has gone missing – that sort of thing – mention no names and nothing specific, just in case it is all above board. How's that?'

'OK Mr B, I'll say nothing until I hear from you – and I'll certainly steer clear of Mr Wilkinson.'

'Same goes for you, Whacker.'

'Course, Dad. I wouldn't want to get involved if that bit we saw turned out to be the real Mr W – no way!'

Satisfied with this, Ted got the lads moving again up to the Manor House where he asked Whacker to give him his opinions on the furniture he'd looked at. Whacker had assessed the signs of minor damage or wear and tear, and his recommendations for remedial action were spot on, apart from a couple of instances where 'tricks of the trade' could be applied. All in all, Ted felt that Whacker had done a good job, and told him so.

'Right then, Dad, what about me going for an apprenticeship? Does it look like I'm good enough, cos if so, I need to get a move on getting something sorted before term starts, right?'

'I'd tell you to stop saying "right", my lad, but in this instance you are right – you're ready for the apprenticeship. Now hold on a mo!' as Whacker jumped up and down in his excitement. 'Before you want to dash off to Bracknell to get your college course sorted, I've got something to sort out here, first. Go and tell Slim and Boots about the apprenticeship, if you like, while I go and find your mum and tell her.'

As Ted approached the cottage, Alison met him smiling happily at what she'd just viewed. 'The cottage is lovely, Ted, but of course there's no garden, no lawn, no veg patch, unless you could have a go on any parts that belong to the big house.'

'Come on, Alison,' he replied, smiling at her opinion. 'Not everybody wants to have an outside job to do when they've finished a full day's work. Surely it'll be nice just to have an evening meal then go out for a walk – through the fields and woods, or up to the village. The main thing is – would you like to be living in this cottage across the yard from my workshop, and only a bus ride from Salchester? Then there's the people up in the village that the lads have talked about, and if Tony Philips is living in the Manor, we'd not be stuck out on our own. But it's got to be a joint decision, and even that has to wait to see what Tony can offer. Let's go up and see him now, OK?'

Not much was happening in the Manor House – all the carpets and furniture were in their allotted places. The Wilkinsons seemed to be in the kitchen and Tony was in the study that, unusually, had its door shut. Boots, Slim and Anna had been looking at the books that came out of the parcels that Slim had carried up from the coach house, but were now listening to an excited Whacker telling them that he was going to be an apprentice cabinetmaker.

Seeing the non-stop questioning he was facing, Ted decided not to interrupt, but took Alison off and knocked on the study door where, after a moment, Tony called them in, again closed the door, and invited them to have a seat.

'Right,' he started, 'if you've had a look at the cottage, are you still interested?'

'Yes, we are, but of course it depends on what's on offer.'

'Well, after that phone call, I'm afraid it's not looking as simple as I'd thought and had hoped,' said Tony. 'And there could be a fair bit to go through, so I hope you don't mind, but I've changed my plans for lunch – instead of going up to the Red Lion, I've asked them to send us some sandwiches and stuff. Then, if we can be quick dealing with your move, I hope you'll still want to spend time on the carriage and the furniture repairs.'

'Oh yes, I'm still up for those things, but you make it sound as if there could be problems with us moving my business here.'

'OK, well I'll just send the others up to the village for a bite to eat, and we can crack on.' Going outside he called Anna, 'I've got things to talk about here, love, so will you take the lads and the Wilkinsons up to the Red Lion for a light lunch, please? They're expecting you. Give us an hour or so.'

Coming back into the study, he started again. 'As I said, it's not looking as simple as I'd thought and any move won't be as quick as you'd suggested.' Seeing Ted and Allison look at each other as if their dream had ended, he continued quickly, 'but there's good news as well as the not so good.'

'Let's have the bad stuff first,' jumped in Alison, 'and if it's too bad for us, you needn't go into what's supposed to be good.' And her expression showed how disappointed she was at Tony's words.

'Right, well, the bad stuff is that it's going to be a little while before anything can happen, and another bad bit is that it's all going to cost a bit more than I'd hoped. Now, do you want me to go on and tell you the good bits, or have I killed the idea for you?'

'No, we're still interested, so carry on and perhaps explain what's changed or what's going to happen.'

'As you might expect, it's the legal people that's put their oar in, but it all makes sense – for once! First off, I'd not thought that it mattered that I'd be "changing the use of the premises" as they call it – but it does, and I'd have to get some permissions. But the real problem is how to separate the main house from the remaining buildings both physically and functionally.'

'Not sure I'm with you,' interrupted Alison.

'Well, up to now, the whole set-up here has been classed as a country house with outbuildings. To operate as we've discussed, and as I'd like to do anyway, it would become a 'house with adjacent independent premises'. Not sure if those were the words he used, but that's my understanding of it. Anyway, to make it workable, it would be simpler if each outbuilding was connected separately to the mains services – water and electricity – because at the moment that all comes via the main house. As far as the electricity is concerned, each outbuilding needs to be properly wired and metered, and so on.'

'So, what's the solution?' asked Ted.

'The only safe solution is for the electrics for each property to be checked out and fitted and upgraded to suit whatever it may be used for.'

'That doesn't sound too bad, just for the coach houses,' said Ted.

'You're right, Ted, but of course that's just looking at what your immediate interest is – but when I said each outbuilding, that's what I meant. That would then cope with you perhaps changing the number of buildings you needed, and so on.'

At this point Tina arrived with their picnic lunch, and the break they took to serve them gave time for them to consider the new, unexpected situation.

'What sort of time scale, do you know yet?' asked Alison.

'No, I've not had time to get quotes, but the people that the estate agency deals with reckons it will be a couple of months at the very least.' Seeing their expressions, Tony quickly carried on, 'But while that is happening, I think it would also be a good idea to do some improvements to the water supply system, not least to perhaps update the bathroom and perhaps add a shower room to the cottage.'

'Now that *would* be worth waiting for!' Alison replied, smiling at last.

'Still interested, then?'

'If the delay is the total of the bad bits, then yes, we are. But didn't you say something about costs going up?' asked Ted.

"Fraid so. As you'll imagine, none of this work is going to be for free and I'll have to recoup it over the years through higher rents. But, apart from that increase, I can't yet get any ideas on what business rates may be imposed and, as far as the cottage is concerned, there'll be Council Tax to pay.'

'We're already used to business rates and Council Tax, so I can check on how this area compares with Bracknell. So, Tony, I'm pretty sure we're still interested. The ambience here is just what I could do with, and I think Alison is getting more into feeling that way. So, where do we stand?'

'If this whole thing was being done purely on the basis of your interest, you'd be asked for a holding deposit but, as I've decided it's the best thing for me to do anyway, I can acknowledge your part in getting me started by offering you first refusal, and also by consulting with you on the improvements as they crop up. How does that sound?'

'That sounds OK, but you've not said anything about what uses you expect to make of the other outbuildings – would there be anything to conflict with my line of business?' asked Ted.

'I'm not talking to anybody else, at all. But the agent has told me about some of the enquiries he got before I bought the estate, and a couple of them might still be interested – that was to set up craft workshops and a sales shop in the stables, plus a tea room sort of thing based in what I now know was the original laundry room. I guess these are the sort of ventures I've pictured here.'

'Oh dear,' was Alison's response.

'What's wrong with that, love?' asked Ted. 'Surely other activities will bring company as well as other possible business for me?'

'That's true all right, but just think where these places are – opposite ends of the yard, with us in the middle, and our paths crossing all the time!'

Ted couldn't help burst out laughing. 'For Heaven's sake, love, you make it sound like Piccadilly Circus!'

'Ah, but your wife's got a point, Ted. I'd not thought about it, but we'd not want the tea shop and craft shop customers getting in the way of your suppliers etc. If you wouldn't want the laundry building yourselves, I'll have to think of a different use for it.'

'Not as straightforward as we'd thought, is it?' remarked Ted, looking very thoughtful and rather despondent. 'Look, Mr Philips, if my needs are going to cause real problems and not fit in with your plans, the sooner you let me know, the better, and I'll knock it on the head and stay in Bracknell.'

'I can't imagine it's as difficult as that, Ted, but I reckon we all need to have a further look at it on the ground. So, what say we go for a walk around together after we've polished off these lovely sarnies.'

So that's what happened.

Chapter 19

The Red Lion was fairly busy but the arrivals from the Manor House were soon seated under a brolly at a table in the Beer Garden, and their conversations continued.

It was easy for Mrs W to excuse herself and go off in search of hubby, soon finding that he'd told Tina that he was going into Salchester but would be back before tea. Somewhat mystified, she went up to their room and discovered that a bag and some of his clothes were missing. She started to panic, then remembered him saying that, before they moved on, he wanted to get some dry-cleaning done at a place they'd always used in Salchester – problem solved.

Downstairs again she almost bumped into Slim heading out of the front door. 'Not eating, young man?' she asked.

'Oh yes, just had a quick bite, but I need to see if Eileen has heard yet from my mother to say when she's arriving. Sorry, but got to go before I miss her.' And off he trotted.

However, when Slim found Eileen at home – she didn't go out with the library on Wednesday afternoons – it was to ask her if she knew how he could contact Detective Cole. He needed to do it quickly and in confidence, and certainly not in the Lion in the evening.

'The best thing is to go to his house – if he's not there, his wife will probably be able to get in touch with him for you – and she's totally reliable and discrete. You know where the house is, don't you, from Sunday evening?'

'Not sure I took much notice, really, but I seem to remember it didn't seem far out.'

'No, it's not. Go back towards the green then take the path on the right just after Mrs Baker's place. That takes you to The Crescent, and the police house is on your right, number 15 – and you'll not be in the sight of anybody from the Red lion, if that's what you want. But before you dash off, your mum phoned and asked if you could stay another night and she'll come for you tomorrow – I said OK, all right? Oh, and when you've done this afternoon, will you want some tea with me and Graham?'

'Thanks, Eileen, that'd be good. But I don't know how long I'll be today, so can't say when to expect me. If I'm likely to be very late, I'll let you know, OK?'

Taking her nod and wave as agreement, Slim was soon along the path, into The Crescent and knocking on DC Cole's front door, all the while trying to act normally, but dreading being seen by Mr, or even by Mrs, W.

The young woman who opened the door didn't seem surprised to see him and invited him inside.

'Hello, you must be Slim,' she greeted him. 'I don't think you saw me on Sunday evening, but I got the gist of what happened to you, and it seems like it was quite useful. So, what can we do for you now?'

'Oh, right, well,' he stumbled, 'it's nothing to do with that and I guess DC Cole will think I'm wasting police time, but I just feel it's important, and I'd like to speak to him, please.'

'Well he's not here right now, but I can try to get him on the phone if it's too urgent to wait till he gets home this evening?'

'Yes, please, if it's not too much trouble.'

Mrs Cole took him into a small office, and dialled a number she obviously knew by heart. 'Hello, is DC Cole available, please? Somebody here needs to speak to him ... Yes, I'm sure he wouldn't mind that.'

Covering the mouthpiece, she told Slim that her husband was with his boss, but that they both generally accepted any interruption that she asked for.

'Hello, love. Sorry to disturb you but I've got the young man you were dealing with on Sunday, name of Slim, and says he needs to speak to you ASAP. Can I put him on? ... OK, here he is.' And she handed the phone over.

'Hello, Mr Cole, this has nothing to do with the thing on Sunday, but I reckon there's some thieving going on here at Charlford Manor.' And he went on to describe the incident with Mr Wilkinson and what he felt sure was a jewellery box. As he finished, feeling it was all rather lame, he was more than a bit surprised with DC Cole's response.

'That's just what we wanted to hear, young man. You see, somebody just now tried to sell some items that he said he'd just found, but they were reported missing many years ago, so we're trying to pin down where he said he found them. Could be that the two are connected, and I think the boss has just given me the nod to come and look at things on the ground. Where can I find the owner of the Manor House, and where will you be?'

'Well, if it's our Mr Wilkinson you're talking about, and if he's not coming back to the Manor this afternoon, I'll go down there – and that's where you'll find the owner, Mr Philips. I'll see if there's anything I can do – have a jam session with the lads or something, it's all a bit disorganised.'

'We don't want anybody to think you've been an informant, so you go to the Manor House in your own time and I'll see you there along with all the rest – and thanks again.'

Ringing off, Slim felt relieved that he didn't seem to be wasting police time, so he thanked Mrs Cole for her help and left to wander slowly back to the Manor House wondering where this could all go. He'd just realised that, whatever Mr W was involved in, the chances were that his wife was too, and Slim didn't like that idea at all – Mrs W had always seemed so nice, kind and friendly.

Finding himself to be the first back from the lunch break, Slim was tempted to look again at where he thought the jewel box had been hidden, but he'd read enough detective novels to know he could easily spoil any evidence. So he went to the stable block to have a closer look at the drum kit that Whacker had been given – Lucky sod, he thought. Actually, it was starting to look like a decent bit of kit, and that made Slim wonder if it really suited the band, after all. Ah well, he thought, burn that bridge when we get to it.

'Hey, Slim!' exclaimed Boots, the first to arrive back. 'What happened to you? We've been looking for you up at the Lion'

'Just went to see Eileen, and she's heard from my mum – she's coming down tomorrow, so I'll be off home then – but not straight off. She wants to meet the people that have helped out during this week – and, you know, I've just realised this weekend will have turned into almost a week. Can't really believe all that's happened, particularly Whacker, of all people, being given a full set of drums! Have you seen the job he's making of cleaning it up?'

'I know, but I reckon it'll be too big for the band to use, don't you?'

Slim was nodding agreement as the others arrived back from the village and began asking Tony what needed to be done next, as if they were extended family or co-workers.

'Well, I need to have a word with Mr Bailey about the coach and some furniture repairs and that's really just about it, unless anybody wants to open up a couple of those parcels and see what the books are like – but I don't want them all unpacking until I decide what to do with them, so please try not to make a mess after all the work you've done in helping to get things straight.'

But before any of this could get happen, a police car rolled up, and they all stopped to stare. The driver, a young woman constable, stayed in the car while DC Cole got out and walked over to where Tony and Whacker's dad were standing.

'Yes, officer,' said Tony, 'what can we do for you?'

'Actually it's 'Detective', sir, but I'm looking for the owner of the property.'

'Sorry, Detective. Well, I'm the owner, Tony Philips, so what can I do for you?'

'Well, sir, we've been informed that some long-lost, or even long-ago-stolen, property has recently been recovered from this estate. So we need to establish what happened and see who might have been involved.'

'Wait a minute, Detective. This is all a bit sudden and out of the blue. As far as I'm aware, nothing's been "recovered" as you say. If you can be a bit more precise I might be able to help you, but bear in mind I've only owned the place a few months and only actually lived here for about six weeks – does that fit your time frame?'

'It certainly does, sir. The items concerned were recovered, we believe, just this morning, so we really need to establish who was here then and find out what, if anything, they might have seen, heard, or even been involved in.'

This statement was heard by the whole group and left them open-mouthed, looking questioningly at each other.

'If any of you were here this morning,' he continued, 'my colleague Constable Hill needs to make a note of your names and contact details, find out if you noticed anything unusual happening during the morning. In the meantime, I'd like you, sir, to show me around the property.'

As DC Cole and Tony moved away towards the Manor House, Whacker's dad stopped them. 'Before you go too far, I saw something you might be interested in, but it was in the stable yard – I can show you, if you like.'

'Very good, sir – and you are?'

Tony made the introduction, then they turned and went towards the stable yard. When the coach came into sight, DC Cole stopped in his tracks. 'What a beauty! You don't see many of those around these days. Do you use it, sir?'

'Do me a favour, Detective, I didn't even know I'd got it until last Friday when we unearthed it – but the legal people say it's mine, so you never know!' and laughed.

At this point, Ted described what had happened when he and Whacker had heard the commotion in the first coach house and seen Mr Wilkinson with the small jewel box.

'Right, sir, that seems to confirm the information we already have, so what we need now is signed statements from all three of you, is that OK?'

'Well,' said Ted, 'that's OK for me and my lad as long as I can be with him when he does his, but I'm not sure about

Slim, as he's really on his own here and I think he needs an adult's support.'

'I take your point, sir, but I shouldn't worry about young Mr Bennett – he gave us some real help on another case last weekend. But if he's happy to have you or Mr Philips sit in with him, that's fine by us.'

With that sorted out, DC Cole got on his radio to arrange for the jewel box hiding place to be examined, then cordoned it off with 'scene of crime' tape – 'Just like on TV,' commented Ted.

'Tell me, Mr Philips, how did this group of people happen to be here this week? Is it a house party, or something?'

Tony explained how it had all started with his daughter finding the lads in the hay field, asking them to play at her party, and so on.

'But what about the two ladies out there?' DC Cole asked.

'Well, there's Mrs Bailey, Ted's wife – they were here on Sunday and again today, just for the day – I've asked Ted to fix some bits of furniture and give me an idea on the state of the coach. The other lady is Mrs Wilkinson – her husband should be around somewhere – they used to work here many years ago and wanted to have another look at the place before they go off somewhere to retire – I think that's right. They just happened to arrive the same day as the lads – and they've both been a great help this week, particularly over the weekend.'

'If Mrs Wilkinson worked here some years ago, then I definitely need to have a word with her, and I'm sure my boss will too, so I'll want to take her back to Salchester. I'll go and have a word with her, if you'll excuse me.'

'But why just her? What about her husband, he worked here at the same time.'

'Don't worry, Mr Philips, we're already talking to her husband – he was the one who has the property we're talking about!'

This news really hit Tony who'd grown fond of the couple, apart from appreciating all the help they'd given over the weekend.

'Wait a mo, Detective. Where are you actually taking her? I feel she'll need somebody there with her – I'm sure she has no idea what's happening and I want her to have some support. I can't get away just yet, myself, but there's a friend in town I'm sure I can get to be with her. Would that be OK?'

'Well, she's not being charged with anything at the moment and I think she probably won't be, so I can't see her needing a solicitor, but if there was somebody nearby for her to turn to, that would be OK. Just call the Police HQ and give them a name and refer them to me – I'll look out for them, OK?'

'I'm hoping it will be Lynda Harris...' but was cut off before he could finish.

'We know Lynda alright, she's helped out before when family liaison has been a bit stretched – wait a minute, are you the Philips of Harris and Philips? We heard you'd sold up and left the area.'

'Yes, it is me and I have part sold up – to Reg Harris, of course – and this is as far as I got in leaving the area,' replied Tony with a smile.

'I'd like to catch up with you later, if I may, sir?' And off he went to find Mrs W without giving Tony any opportunity to argue or bargain with him.

'Wow, Ted, that's a turn up. Now let's see that the rest are OK. I'm sure the youngsters knew nothing that will help the police, so we can perhaps get on with our own business after I've made this call to see if Lynda can be there to support Mrs W.'

'Well, my wife and I still need to put Whacker in the picture on our thoughts about the move – and see if he's got any input, of course. So, we'll do that and come up to the house in ten mins or so, OK?'

And so it was that, with Mrs W and Slim off in the police car, and Whacker and his parents off into the stable yard for a serious chat, Boots at last found himself alone with Anna.

'Are there any more jobs to do for your dad?' he asked, hoping there'd be something to keep her attention and interest.

'I think we deserve a break, don't you? You guys have really been a great help to us this week – and it's not what you came to the village for, is it?'

'It's hard to say what we came for, really. We only said the other evening that we'd not known what to expect it to be like, apart from not having to lug our kit around, cook for ourselves, and probably get cold and wet at night.' Her lovely light laugh encouraged him to continue, 'And I never expected to meet someone like you.' Then he stopped and blushed.

Anna wasn't surprised at his words, but didn't want to encourage him and just didn't know what to say, but the moment was gone when Whacker burst into the open from the coach house area – 'Hey, Boots, Anna, guess who might be coming to live here and work with his dad!!'

'Father Christmas,' replied Anna with a chuckle.

'Not you, mate, surely!' was Boots' response. 'What about the band and college and... and...?'

'Yes, me, mate. My mum and dad are hoping to move here so Dad can have his workshop here and take me on as an apprentice cabinetmaker and I'd go to college in Salchester and – but it won't happen just yet. So, yes, sorry about the band. Oh, and we'll have to sort out with Tony what I'm supposed to do with the drum kit now.'

'Is it all fixed then?' asked Anna, who'd known from her dad that it was a possibility.

'Sort of, I think. I mean, we're probably definitely coming to live and work here, but there's got to be some work done on the buildings first and then they've got to decide if it's permanent, like, or not, like.' And he ran out of steam but not out of excitement.

Just then, Ted and Alison came past on their way to the main house. 'I guess he's told you, then?' asked Alison, rather unnecessarily. 'But until we've got things agreed with your dad, Anna, we don't know exactly when the move will happen. With the building work that's got to be done, it definitely won't be before the next college term starts, so it gives time for that to be sorted out.'

So, Boots' time alone with Anna was again cut short, and the three of them roamed rather aimlessly around the stable yard, then the front lawn of the house, and finally along the path towards the village, analysing events of the past week and wondering what the future might bring.

Chapter 20

Anna, Boots and Whacker had arrived at the Red Lion feeling warm and ready for the cool drinks that Tina served them at a table under a shade in the Beer Garden. She wasn't really on duty and happily joined them while they got her up to speed with all that had happened at the Manor House that afternoon. And none of them was sure which was the hottest topic – the stolen jewellery or the prospect of Whacker's move to Charlford Manor estate – but the latter was the one that would affect them most, so that got all the attention.

'But why would your dad want to move here, Whacker?' asked Tina.

'There's nothing wrong with Bracknell,' he started, 'but it's getting bigger and busier and I reckon he's just ready for a change and this is the first place to get his attention. Mind you, that carriage would have lured him in this direction even if he'd not been thinking of a move.'

'What's the carriage got to do with it?' This was Anna, wondering if her dad had come to some arrangement about it without telling her. 'I think it's a real asset to the estate and I thought my dad might do something with it – you know, get a couple of horses to take it around, and so on,' she ended rather lamely.

'I don't think my dad's got any designs on it, apart from getting the chance to study how it was put together and perhaps do any repair work on it. I think he just likes it being there.'

'And that's enough reason to consider moving his works and your family home here?' joined in Boots, who was more than a bit miffed that Whacker might be moving in next door to Anna while he, Boots, was stuck in Bracknell. After all, Whacker already had his eye on Tina – how many girlfriends did he need, let alone deserve?

'Look, it's hard to explain and I can't properly answer for my dad, but he and Mum perhaps just want a quieter lifestyle. You girls are probably so used to it you don't realise how nice it is here – in the heart of the country but just a bus ride from the city. You've got it made, and I'm really looking forward to the move – if it comes off of course – and finding my way around properly.'

'But make sure you steer clear of the likes of the bloke that duffed up poor old Slim,' added Boots, 'that's not part of your country idyll.'

'Oh yes, I know it wouldn't be all sweetness and light, but I'm really looking forward to it.'

Before this discussion could go any further, though it would probably have gone around in circles, they heard a car draw up at the front of the inn and Tina's dad greeting Mrs W. Tina went through to the front to see if her dad needed her.

'I guess you must be tired, Mrs Wilkinson, so perhaps you'd like a cup of tea in the quiet of the lounge before you go up to your room?'

'I'd love a cup of tea, Mr Parker, but I just couldn't face that room. I'm sorry, but after how that man has used and treated me, I want nothing more to with him or anything he's touched or had dealings with.'

And with that, Mrs W put her hands to her face, started to sob, and looked as if she might collapse. Tina and her dad stepped forward and, supporting her, helped her into the Residents' Lounge, which fortunately was deserted. Settling her into a comfortable armchair, Jim went to fetch the tea he'd promised while Tina knelt beside her, tried to comfort her, and motioned the others not to come in when they appeared in the doorway.

Boots and Anna had heard nothing about Mr W's verbal attack on Slim, so Whacker was able to put them in the picture. Mrs W's outburst seemed to confirm that, while Mr W had been up to no good and had been found out, it seemed that Mrs W was ignorant of his activities and therefore an innocent victim.

'But they seemed such a lovely couple,' was all Anna could say.

'I know,' added Whacker. 'They reminded me of my Uncle Jim and Auntie Joan, and I took to them from the start. I wonder what will happen now.'

'One thing that's got to happen,' said Anna, becoming very practical, 'is Mrs W has to have somewhere to sleep tonight. I can understand her not wanting to share that bedroom again, assuming her husband comes back tonight.'

'But what can we do?' the lads asked together.

'Well I'm going to ring my dad and see if we can offer Mrs W a bed for the night, and if we can, you two can help get her luggage down to the house – OK?'

'Sure thing, boss!' quipped Whacker, earning a dig in the ribs from Boots – he wasn't happy seeing Whacker get too familiar with Anna!

Left on their own, Boots took the opportunity to find out more about the Bailey family's planned move to Charlford.

'What would you do about school?' he asked. 'And what about the band? And there's the set of drums and...' he'd run out of things to query, but felt there was much more needed explaining.

'I know it's a lot to take in – it is for me as well – but it all seems to fit into place. Dad is taking me on as an apprentice, right? But I've got to carry on at college to get the right supporting qualifications, and I could transfer to Salchester and carry on with it there – Dad's already been in touch and we're going for an interview sort of thing tomorrow. And it should be great. But of course, the novelty will wear off and I'll miss you and Slim and the music, but there's bound to be something I can get into here.'

'Perhaps join the cathedral choir?' laughed Boots. 'But, come on, you're going to be under your dad's eagle eye most of the time, and you'll need to get off into the woods and fields for a walk and a lark about, and how's that going to be on your own? I reckon you'll miss us more than you think.'

'You may be right, but it's a family decision and I'm in the minority, so even if I didn't want to move – and I do – I'd have no option. And anyway, Bracknell's not a million miles away. If one of you can put me up for a night or two I reckon

I can come along for a meet-up some time. And you know what the accommodation's like down here, so you'd both always be welcome.'

This opening up had made them both realise the enormity of what could soon be happening and had made them think seriously about it. But it was Whacker who brought the conversation back to the present.

'Of course, Dad and Tony still have to finalise the details, and it still may not work out. But even if the move doesn't happen, Dad's still taking me on as an apprentice – magic!!'

'Does Slim know all about this?' asked Boots.

'Do you know, I don't think he does. He keeps sloping off to do his own thing and I'm not sure what he's heard or knows about it.'

'I know what you mean,' replied Boots. 'He's nipped off now with no word about when he'll be back. You'd never think this whole weekend started off as his idea and his PLAN!!' And they both laughed.

Just then, Anna returned to say her dad was offering Mrs W the spare room in the cottage, so the lads' kind offer to help move her luggage would be taken up – but she couldn't face going up to her room to pack just yet.

'What about my mum and dad?' asked Whacker. 'Is there enough room for them in the cottage as well?'

'No, but they're with Dad right now and he checked that they're happy to have one of the rooms over the stables that I used with the girls last weekend. So, it's all sorted – and Mrs W is SO grateful to you for your kind offer to help with her luggage!' she ended with a laugh.

'What happens now, then?' asked Boots, turning to Anna. 'Looks like Slim's off at an evening meal at Eileen's, Whacker here has got to meet up with his folks to find out what's happening about this school interview tomorrow, and you're sorting out a bed for the night for the Bailey family – leaves me feeling like a bit of a spare part.'

'Ah! Poor lamb! You really mustn't feel you're not wanted – there's Mrs W's luggage to get down to the Manor House as soon as she's packed it – and if you're good you can walk there beside me instead of two paces behind like a common surf!!' And the smile she bestowed on poor Boots took away any worries he had about losing her affections – slight as they probably were. 'And unless Dad's come up with some amazing idea for dinner, it looks like we'll all be eating back here later on, OK?'

'Fine by me, so let's see about this luggage I'm expected to lug! – Did the word "lug" came from luggage, I wonder?'

(*To save you checking, dear reader, my dictionary says the derivation may be the other way round, i.e., 'luggage' perhaps comes from 'heavy things to lug' – I know what they mean!*)

Chapter 21

Jim Parker and his staff at the Red Lion hadn't had as many bookings as this for a single meal since Mothering Sunday, and were almost run off their feet, mainly because it was all fairly spontaneous. However, although it was the party from the Manor House that had caused the last-minute worries, they were treated just the same as Ted's regular guests, and all were well satisfied with the service as well as with the meal itself – in fact they rather relished the longer-than-usual breaks between servings as it gave them chance to talk, and they really did have a lot to talk about.

Mrs Wilkinson was persuaded to join them, though she said she really couldn't face eating and felt so embarrassed about her husband's behaviour.

'I'm so sorry Mr Philips, but I assure you I knew nothing about the jewellery. Well that's not quite right because I do vaguely remember a fuss some years ago when I worked here; some items went missing and weren't found, and I seem to remember something about an insurance claim, but that's all.'

Slim had arrived by this time and was able to fill in a few details that he'd picked up from the police. 'It seems that nobody in the family could say exactly when the items had gone missing – they weren't used that often – and suspicion seemed to finally land on the butler who'd been sacked and had left in a hurry. But he'd moved a few times and couldn't be found, and the police soon put the case on the back burner, as you might say.'

'So how come it all came to light today?' asked Tony. 'Not that I'm unhappy about that – at least it's being cleared up fairly quickly, it seems.'

'Well,' resumed Slim, unconsciously slipping into management mode, 'it appears that the family had been advised early on by their insurers to photograph all their valuables, so photos of the lost items were circulated by the police to loads of jewellers, pawn shops and so on. It just so happens that the shop where the items were taken today was where some of them had been bought in the first place. Staff in jewellers always refer to the notices the police send round about lost or stolen items – particularly local items – and the staff in the shop in Salchester contacted the police as soon as they saw them.

'Wow,' interjected Tony, 'that really was a stroke of luck – though bad luck for Mr Wilkinson. But, hang on a minute, surely he could still have simply just found them, couldn't he? Somebody was bound to do that some day – it could even have been me – would I have been hauled in for theft?'

'Don't know about that, Tony, but it was Mr W's fingerprints on one of the items that did for him.'

'Surely that would be the case for whoever found them – you'd naturally handle them, wouldn't you?'

'Of course, but, in this case, one of Mr W's prints had gained a small scar in recent years, but an un-scarred version was on there from way back. But that simply proves that he handled the piece back then and, of course, that would have been possible because of his work here. So it looks like he won't be charged with nicking the stuff but only with handling stolen property – and even then, the police will have to prove he knew it was stolen – or something like that. Anyway, that's really just between us, though I guess much of it will be in tomorrow's local paper.'

'Wow, Slim, you've really got yourself involved in the murky side of the area this week, haven't you?' said Whacker's dad. 'Has it helped with your ideas of joining the police, now you've seen it a bit up close?'

'Oh no, Mr B. The rough stuff last Sunday really knocked that on the head – no pun intended,' though it got quite a laugh. 'I've thought about the legal profession, but I'm sure that can be quite stuffy, so my latest idea...'

'Not another PLAN, is it Slim?' interjected Whacker, with a theatrical moan.

'No, Whacker, just a thought that being a reporter could be good fun – right there near the action, but not really involved. Yes, that sounds good.'

'Well, you certainly seemed to give us a good summing-up of what's been happening, Slim, so pay no attention to this offspring of mine and follow your instincts, and good luck to you.' A heartfelt statement that was met with nods and comments of agreement that made Slim feel really pleased until he realised Mrs W had been sitting there quietly all the time he'd been reporting on her husband's misdeeds. And he wasn't the only one to realise they'd perhaps been less than kind in their comments, and Mrs W. recognised this and spoke up.

'I know how you all must feel about my husband, and I want you all to know, as I've already said, that I knew nothing about the stolen jewellery, and I'm truly ashamed of his actions, particularly after the kindness we've both enjoyed during the past few days. It may seem that just handling these goods is a fairly minor crime compared with stealing them as well. But, in my book, it is totally unacceptable and I'll do whatever I can to help – I don't know – to put things right? I certainly want nothing more to do with Mr W – I'll just have to find a way to carry on on my own. And I'll be out of your hair, Mr Philips, as soon as I can sort my affairs, if you can bear to have me around for a few days.'

'Don't worry yourself, Mrs W, there's no rush for you to move on, and if Anna and I can help in any way, you must ask – after all that you've done for us these past few days, it's the least we can do.'

With that, Mrs W sat back and seemed to shrink a little while the rest of them all felt a little embarrassed for her predicament. After a minute or so, conversations picked up again when Anna asked her dad how things were looking with the possible move of the Bailey family.

'Unfortunately, the more I look into things, the more problems seem to crop up, though nothing so serious that we're dropping the idea, it's just that it looks like it will all take longer because of the necessary works – and that, of course will put up the initial costs and then the eventual rentals etc.'

'Is this putting you off, Dad?' asked Whacker, wondering if the whole idea of his apprenticeship might be in danger.

'Well, no, not at all, as long as Tony's eventual solution suits our needs, and that should work out all right because he's asked me to help with the plans etc. No, lad, it just might be a bit longer before we look at a move from Bracknell – and don't worry about the apprenticeship, that's going ahead wherever we are.'

'Come on, Dad,' continued Anna, 'can't you let us in on any of it? Surely a few more heads might come up with some answers.'

'Well,' he began, 'as you know, Ted wants one – and perhaps two – of the coach houses as a workshop plus the staff cottage to live in. That leaves the laundry room – for want of a better name – available for some other use, but it sits right between the cottage and the coach houses. Now the agents tell me that the only people that have been interested in coming to the estate wanted to use the laundry room for a kitchen to prepare teas etc. for a café/teashop they wanted to put in the stables. So that would result in foot traffic going corner to corner of the stable yard, right across the front of the cottage – and if they can't get the cottage to live in, I don't think Ted would be interested in the coach house.'

'I think you should stop right there, Dad.' Anna jumped in so quickly, and rather loudly, that it got everybody's attention. 'Some of you know Debs, right, one of what Dad calls the Alphabet girls?'

She got nods all round, though none of the lads could remember which girl was which.

'Well,' she continued, 'her parents have a nice big garden and a couple of times a year they open it for the National Garden Scheme, OK? Well Debs reckons it's not worth being there on those days, with all the visitors and their families roaming round, looking in the house windows as well as at the garden. It seems to me that, while it would be fine for any trades and crafts people to have their own customers and suppliers visiting, I'm sure you wouldn't want to create what they call a visitor attraction.'

'Spot on, Anna, and thanks for bringing it up – not something I'd thought of,' replied Tony.

'I must say I'd be happier without members of the public being free to roam around,' joined in Ted, 'mainly because of the safety aspects of my machinery, but also when I'm doing repairs on customers' pieces – a big responsibility.'

'Well that settles it for me, and I think you've summarised it very well,' Tony said, with some relief in his voice. 'No access for the public, but just provision of parking and washrooms for suppliers and invited customers – much easier to cater for. Right, we are making progress.'

'But now that Mr Bailey has mentioned machinery, Dad, what will it be like to have that noise in the background when we're at home? Sorry, Mr Bailey, but the Manor House will still be our home and I've no idea what any of your machinery will sound like, or when you'd need to use it.' Anna felt awkward about mentioning her concerns but, after all, it was Mr Bailey who'd raised the subject.

Ted jumped in before an embarrassed-looking Tony could comment – 'Don't worry, Anna, but you were right to raise it. All I can say is that most of our work is with hand tools, with very little hammering, and I'd happily keep any power-tool work to any period of the day that suited, subject to being free to ask for exceptions to be agreed. And Mrs B certainly won't accept any more noise nuisance than necessary, will you love?' he asked

'Certainly not,' his wife agreed, firmly enough to raise a few smiles amongst the group.

'Well I think that's about as far as we can go until I get some idea of planning approvals and works costings so, when we've all finished our meals, let's see about getting Mrs Wilkinson settled in the cottage. No need for you lads to carry luggage, thanks, we'll take it with Mrs W in the car.'

'Can I walk you home, Anna?' asked Boots hopefully.

'Sorry, Boots, but I'm helping get Mrs W settled in – though I should be ready for a bit of a stroll in about half an hour, if anybody was around to keep me company!' And she headed off to give Mrs W a hand, leaving a quietly-smiling Boots in her wake.

'Right, you two,' began Ted, 'time for us to get along to the Manor House as well and see about finding our way around the stable block – by the way, where's young Slim? He seemed to just disappear after his chat about the stolen jewels – hope all's OK.'

'Don't worry about him, Dad, he'll have had his dinner with Eileen and Graham and probably stayed on for more tuition in the noble art of Crib! He tells us he's really taken to it, but he's not tried to involve me and Boots yet, so I can't tell you any more about it.'

'Crib, eh? Used to enjoy the odd game of that but couldn't match the speed of the old boys in totting up their scores – must have another go at it some time.'

'Don't let Graham hear you say that unless you really mean it and have a few hours to spare – according to Slim, that is.'

'Anyway, that's enough for one day, I think, so we'll be off. See you in the morning and let's get some of those repairs seen to.'

'Goodnight, Mum. Goodnight Dad.'

'Goodnight, son.'

And with that, Boots and Whacker went upstairs, carried Mrs Wilkinson's luggage down to Tony's car, and found themselves adrift and at a bit of a loss as to what to do next. It was far too early to turn in and, anyhow, Boots had an offer of a late evening stroll with Anna, while Whacker hoped for a walk, perhaps down to the ford, with Tina as soon as she finished helping her dad.

'Fancy a run-through of any of our stuff, Whacker?'

'Not really, not without Slim – and it's odd, you know, to sort of miss the bossy so-and-so.'

'Well this whole week's been a bit odd – there's been times when I've had a job remembering what brought us here. The Acolytes have certainly taken a back seat in my thoughts – and the band really must be a low priority for you to be happy about moving down here, away from me and Slim.'

'Hell, yes. And I'm really sorry if it looks like I'm not bothered, but getting an apprenticeship has always been my main hope, and doing it with my dad is the icing on the cake – it's just sad that it's got to be away from you guys. I'll miss you both, and not just for the music, though I guess that without it we'd not have much in common.'

'Guess you're right, but, hey, here comes young Tina, and I'd better be off for my walk out with Anna. See you later – and not too late, big day tomorrow.'

And so they went their separate ways for gentle strolls in the warm dusk air.

Chapter 22

Alison Bailey woke slowly, wondering for a moment where she was. Ted's line of work had made it difficult to get away for holidays so she wasn't used to waking up in strange beds in strange rooms. Catching sight of Ted, gazing out of the low window, brought it all back to her – they were in one of the rooms above the stables at Charlford Manor – and they were hoping, indeed planning, to move here to live and work. This realisation sent a thrill though her and she called out a cheery 'Good morning'. To her shocked surprise her husband just didn't respond.

'What's the matter, Ted?' she asked. 'What's bothering you?'

'I think I've blown it, love,' he replied, turning to face her. 'I think I've well and truly blown it!'

'Oh, come on, love, nothing can be as bad as that. What's bothering you?'

'Give me a minute to make us a cup of tea and I'll tell you,' he replied, leaving the room to go to the small kitchen at the end of the corridor. They'd both been agreeably surprised at how compact and functional this loft area was – designed for the benefit of the stables staff, then cleaned up and modernised for use by house guests such as Anna's friends during her birthday weekend.

'Come on and sit down and tell me all about it,' Alison almost commanded when he returned. 'I can't believe things are as bad as you seem to think.'

'No, love, you come here and look out of the window and tell me what you see,' he replied.

'Why, there's nothing, is there? Nice and clean area, no rubbish, no loose animals. What am I supposed to be seeing?'

'The fact that you're seeing nothing is the answer. You should be seeing that carriage, in all its glory. So my concern is – where has it gone? And who took it? And when?'

'Well, it wasn't there when we came in last night, so it must have been moved earlier.'

'That's right, but we were all up at the Red Lion having dinner, so none of us moved it.'

'But why does it bother you so much, love. It isn't our coach, now, is it?'

'No, but it was me that got Tony to move it out of the coach house so I could have good look at it, and I should have made sure it was put away afterwards – so it's my responsibility. How is he now going to trust me with anything? How can he let me take away those pieces of his furniture to repair at home? And how could he happily let us rent the cottage and workshop if he wasn't confident we'd look after it all properly? I tell you, love, that simple oversight has ruined everything.' And Ted really looked like the unhappiest man on earth.

Alison found it hard to believe it all was as black as Ted had painted it, but just didn't know what to say to him and they stood there in silence. This was at last broken by a cheery call from Anna standing outside the cottage – 'Come on you two, breakfast in two minutes.'

'Best get a move on and face the music, I suppose,' said Ted, who couldn't really face eating breakfast – or even eating anything at that moment.

'It'll be all right, love,' replied Alison as she hurried off to the bathroom, leaving Ted to quickly dress and pack his overnight things ready for the early departure he expected.

Arriving in the cottage kitchen a few minutes later they got a warm welcome from Tony, asking if they'd been comfortable and had slept well. He gave no sign that he was aware that the carriage had gone, and Alison hoped it would stay that way until they'd eaten, but Ted, being the Ted she knew, just had to raise the subject.

'Look, Tony, I think we ought to sort out the carriage problem, don't you? I know you've been busy looking after Mrs Wilkinson, but I assume you realise the carriage has gone?'

'No, Ted, I didn't know – I've not been out there yet. Did they smash the lock?'

'I assume so, if there was a lock on the wheels.'

'No, I mean the lock on the coach house door.'

'Do you mean it was in the coach house last night?' asked a relieved-looking Ted.

'Well, yes. Where did you think it was?'

'I didn't know it had been put away, so I thought somebody had nicked it from the yard while we were up in the village.'

They both laughed at their misunderstanding, but Ted suggested they go over to the coach house to check and be sure it was there. They did, and it was, so they got on with their breakfasts in a more relaxed mood.

Meanwhile, up in the village, Slim met up with Boots and Whacker as they left the Red Lion after breakfast, all three wondering what the day would bring. There was no indication that Tony Philips needed them to help with more work at the Manor House, but Whacker thought he'd be helping his dad with some small furniture repair jobs, and Slim expected his mum to turn up during the morning and would probably want him to go home with her.

All this left Boots feeling decidedly left out. 'It looks like we could all be off in different directions this morning! Can't we do something about it?'

They both looked at him a bit puzzled – their own situations had so totally absorbed them that they'd each neglected the others. It was Slim, in management mode again, that was first to spot the problem and see possible solutions.

'I guess none of us needs to be here after today, so I reckon you could come home with me and my mum, or with Whacker and his folks. Is that what you mean?'

'Well, yes, I suppose so, but it all seems a bit limp and – I don't know – we've done some interesting stuff, but none of it was what we came for, and here we are just drifting off home. At least if we'd been going by bus we'd have had that time together – it almost feels like the break-up of the band. Or is it just me?'

'Oh, mate!' said Whacker. 'I've been so wrapped up in plans for moving, working with my dad and so on – I can see how you – and Slim – might feel. But look, we don't have to go home with family today, do we? We're still booked in here and can go home on the bus tomorrow. What about you, Slim? Could you stay over, do you think?'

'Oh, I reckon Graham would have me stay like a shot, if only to have a few more hands at Crib, but my mum's coming to get me and, of course, I don't know what she'll need to give Eileen for my board money – but it's worth an ask. How about you then, Boots?'

'Well, it would suit me to stay – spend a bit more time with Anna this evening, perhaps – in fact, now you mention it, she reckoned one of those tapestries hanging in the hall might be worth more of a look at. Yes, I could easily find something useful to do. It all hangs on you then, Slim – if you can stay we can all go home on the bus tomorrow and it won't waste our tickets. What about it?'

'You two go on down to the Manor House and I'll see you and tell you what's happening when I bring my mum down to meet Tony. OK?'

With the immediate problem solved, Boots and Whacker went off to the Manor House, leaving Slim hanging around the Red Lion waiting for his mum to arrive and wondering how on earth he could broach the idea of not going home with her after she'd driven all that way to collect him. He was nowhere near deciding this when his thoughts were interrupted by his mum's car as it pulled up. At the same time, landlord Jim appeared with the blackboard listing the day's meal specials, so Slim was able to make the introductions.

'Ah,' said Jim with a smile, 'Mrs Bennett, the famous musicians' agent! Pleased to meet you at last.'

'I'm so sorry about that deception,' replied Sarah, feeling her face redden, 'and I'm equally sorry for the problems he brought you and grateful for the help you gave him. It's so unlike him to get into any sort of trouble, or I'd never have tried to make the booking.'

'Oh, don't worry, I was only joking. They're a grand set of lads and have caused me no direct problems – and they've been a real help to Tony Philips along at the Manor House. But enough gossiping out here, let me offer you some refreshment after your journey.' And he led her inside, leaving Slim still wondering how he could suggest he might stay another night. But, as he followed them inside, he found he needn't have worried because Jim was raising the subject. 'I must admit,' he was saying, 'I'd wondered if they might be as little trouble as you'd suggested on the phone but, in the event, we've heard not a peep of music from them. And, of course, we won't now, with you taking your son home today.'

'Are the others still here?' she asked. 'You must think me awful, but I've absolutely no idea what's been happening these past few days – I just assumed the others had gone home as planned and that Peter was still here on his own.'

So, Jim and Slim told her all about what had happened, Slim laying it on a bit thick about them all spending time and energy in helping others and not leaving enough time to themselves for just chatting and practising their music. If he'd been going home with them on the bus in the morning that would have been good, but he fully understood his mum's need to come and meet the people who'd helped him out over the week.

'Oh dear,' she said, 'well I wouldn't mind you staying overnight if there was somewhere for you to stay, but I'd really hoped for your company on the way home – the roads are quite busy in some places and it's nice to have someone to help me navigate. Never mind, Peter, if we can get somewhere for you to stay I'll be OK going home on my own. Could the people you've been staying with have you for another night, do you think?'

'I don't know, Mum, but we can ask when we go and see them – they're expecting us and I think Eileen's got a spot of lunch for us.'

After a bit more of a relax, that was where they went, had a light lunch, and found that Eileen and Graham were quite happy for Slim to stay another night (and another few hands of Crib!)

After again expressing her thanks for all they'd done for her son, and failing to get Eileen to accept any payment other than the meat token Boots had won in the Tell-a-Tale contest, Slim took his mum along to the Manor House to meet Tony, though it was Whacker's mum they encountered first – Tony had gone into Salchester.

The three lads had become so close through their music that they found it hard to realise that their parents hardly knew each other – at least, that was the case with Slim's mum, probably with him being the oldest of the three. He was more than pleased, therefore, to see how well she got on with Whacker's mum, Alison.

Sarah was fascinated to find that Alison and her family were planning to move to Charlford, on what seemed to be little more than the discovery of the horse-drawn carriage and the opportunity for her husband to move his workshop there! This was not at all how Sarah thought a family should plan and conduct their lives. But, in spite of that, she found Alison easy to talk to and soon found herself confiding in her about how she realised she'd let her son down by not getting here earlier, and now she was trying to make it up to him by arranging for him to stay another night, even though it meant her driving home alone.

'Perhaps I can help there,' said Alison. 'We're going back this evening, so I could travel with you, if you like – just for the company – and my husband will be happy to drive home on his own – give him chance to listen to some sport on the radio! But if you've had enough driving for one day and would like to stay overnight, I'm sure Mr Philips wouldn't mind if I stayed on and you can take me back tomorrow. I think we could make up an extra room for you – and I bet Anna would love the extra company. Between you and me, I think she's going to find it a bit lonely here at weekends, though I gather she's become quite friendly with the young lady at the Red Lion that my lad's rather keen on! Oops, sorry, I'm rambling on again. Think what you'd like to do about going home and I'm sure we can sort something out that suits.'

'That's really kind of you, and I think I'd like to stay if it's at all possible and not too much trouble. I've had a hectic few days and a bit of countryside peace sounds lovely – oh! but I've no night things!'

'We'll worry about that once we know there's somewhere for you to stay. Let's go and find Anna.'

They went into the Manor House, headed for the kitchen as a good place to start looking, and struck lucky as Anna was there preparing things for a salad. After introductions and an explanation of the situation, she said that an extra bed would be no problem, but that Mrs W might not be too happy about meeting Sarah because of Slim's involvement with Mr W's situation. Slim agreed he should keep out of the way, and headed off for the stable yard in the hope that Boots and Whacker were there.

Alison hadn't realised that this was all news to Sarah, so she and Anna quickly described what had happened and they were just finishing when Mrs W came into the kitchen.

She'd obviously overheard enough to realise she was the subject, but immediately put them at ease over it. 'I know this may sound odd,' she said, 'but I'm pleased this thing with my husband came to light now. And as for your son's involvement, all he did was point out where that wretched jewel box came from, so I don't blame him at all. Whether my husband's guilty or not, the sooner it's sorted the better, then we can get on with the rest of our lives, OK?'

'That's very good of you, Mrs Wilkinson, and if I can help in any way, please ask – I'll leave you my phone number before we set off home, hopefully tomorrow rather than tonight, but I really don't have any overnight things.'

'I'm sure we can rustle up some things between us,' said Anna, 'starting with a choice of at least half a dozen pairs of pyjamas that Mum got for Dad! She always found it easier to buy new than to wash and iron what he'd used!'

'Oh, Miss Anna, I'm sure that's an exaggeration,' Mrs W with a rare smile.

'Perhaps, but anyway, there's plenty of choice! Oh, and I can offer a new toothbrush – I'd got it ready for new school term, but I've decided not to board any more. I can go on the bus with Tina from the Red Lion, and Dad really will need someone to be here to keep things ticking over – and if you could stay on a bit, Mrs W, we'd really appreciate any help you could offer – but don't tell Dad I just said that – silly man thinks he can manage!'

And they all burst out laughing, including Mrs W – the first time that Anna had seen this since Mr W's departure and eventual arrest. When they calmed down, Anna finished the salad, popped it into the fridge, then led them all upstairs to a linen cupboard and offered Sarah a choice of pyjamas as promised.

'The toothbrush,' she continued, 'is over in the cottage, so let's go there on the way to sorting out a room above the stables, OK?'

'That's wonderful, but however can I repay you?'

'Well, we're going to be moving to live in the main house as soon as we can get it finally ready,' said Anna. 'It's the turn of the cottage to be done up a bit – and about time too. Only one bathroom and no separate toilet, but it's got a terrific cooker. If you really want to help, I want to get some of our clothes moved over here before the chaps from the removal firm come along to deal with the bigger items.'

Showing the leadership that earned her the role of School Prefect, Anna led the ladies out of the Manor House and round to the stable yard where they were met by the sight and sound of The Acolytes running through 'Autumn Morning' outside the end stable. They paused to listen and gave a genuine and warm round of applause when the piece ended.

'I know it would be a shame for the group to be broken up by us moving away from Bracknell,' said Alison, somewhat wistfully, 'so we've decided we can offer Whacker the chance to stay there in digs for the rest of the school year if he really wants to. But, let's face it, they'll all go their separate ways by this time next year – unless the band were to really take off, of course.'

'That's a big decision to put on a lad's shoulders, Alison, but that's what happens in life, isn't it?

'Well, I think they're good,' interjected Anna, 'but are they good enough to give up plans for other careers? I'm sorry, but I think they're too nice – if that's the right word – for what you hear about the music world. Perhaps I mean they don't seem hard enough. But then again, a decent manager or somebody could perhaps provide that for them – I don't know, but it's going to be a tough decision for somebody.'

Further discussion was interrupted when Tony Philips arrived – Anna introduced him to Sarah and got his approval for her to stay the night.

'Very pleased to be of help, Mrs Bennett. The lads have really brought some life to the place these past few days, and your boy has been a lot of help to the police, I gather – oops, sorry, Mrs W!'

'No offence taken, sir. Mr W deserves whatever comes to him, I'm sure.'

'Yes, but it leaves you in a predicament, so we'll help in any way we can – right, Anna? Anyway, I've really not thanked the lads properly for all their help, so how about we all go to the Red Lion for a meal on me this evening?'

'Oh, Dad! Mrs W has helped me make a quiche for supper and I've just put a salad in the fridge! Do we have to go to the Lion?'

'Now then, love, you know me and my thoughts on salad! Look, how about we split up? If the ladies would like to stay here and share the salad, I'll take the lads to the Lion – I really do need a steak and a beer after my day in town! And I want to have a chat with that detective about site security once the building work starts in the stable yard.'

All concerned seemed happy with the plan and the afternoon drew to a close with the Acolytes refining a couple of lyrics, Tony making some phone calls, and the ladies sorting out beds and showing Sarah around. Finally,

Whacker's dad appeared from the coach house where he'd been quietly polishing a couple of pieces of furniture from the house. After an introduction to Sarah and an update on the travel plans, he got the lads to help him load a couple of drums into his van, then said farewell to Tony and set off for home, hoping to beat some of the teatime traffic.

The evening found the lads somewhat subdued – they enjoyed the meal alright, but they weren't particularly interested in Tony's plans for the stable yard buildings, or his chat with Loada Cole about security.

But then Loada asked again about the carriage, and the chance of it being used. It turned out that one of his colleagues had been with the Met in London and had a go at carriage driving under tuition from staff who drove the Royal carriages. That had made him keen to take it up as a hobby. This got Whacker's interest and he promised to remind his dad to find somebody who could get the carriage overhauled.

Slim tried to move things along as he knew that Graham expected him back early enough for a couple of hands of Crib. But mentioning this resulted in Tony and Loada getting him to give Eileen a call to ask Graham to join them at the Red Lion. Once he arrived and the three men began chatting about Crib – Tony to learn the game, Loada asking about local clubs and leagues and so on – the lads thanked Tony, then made their excuses saying they needed to go and pack, etc.

Of course, they needed very little time to pack and would do it in the morning. So, with unspoken agreement, they drifted off once more to the ford and again stood gazing at the slow-moving waters, lower than usual after a very dry month.

'This really is it, isn't it?' asked Slim, quietly. 'The end, I mean. Our last evening here, and probably anywhere as a band.'

'Gosh, Slim, that sounded real soulful. Haven't we had a great week – apart from you getting belted, of course? We've met some interesting folks – virtually lived in a real Manor

House – me and Whacker met a couple of lovely girls – you made friends with the local constabulary and probably made a real career choice – and all in a week that started off as a weekend!'

'Not forgetting the drum kit,' added Whacker.

'And I'm really pleased for you about that, Whacker,' replied Slim, 'but even without you leaving Bracknell – and I'm OK about that, too – can we really see a future for The Acolytes, beyond what we've done already? It's a hobby, and a very creative one, but I don't think any of us has got the necessary drive for a career in showbiz.' A pause, but neither of the other two looked ready to argue. 'So, come one, we haven't, have we? We're just a bunch of mates and we've written some nice stuff that'll stay with us for probably ever, but we've not performed it beyond a couple of auditions – and none of those sent people absolutely wild.'

'That's a bit of a sorry conclusion, Slim,' replied Boots, 'but I must admit I think I agree, though I hadn't thought it clearly enough to say it outright.'

'Well, for me, Slim,' interjected Whacker, 'if the band does finish, you've made my day saying that we're a bunch of mates. Thanks, and I mean it. I'm younger than you two and I always felt you kind of tolerated me. And what you said about this being the sort of natural end of the band – well that makes me feel easier about moving away – and about keeping the drums!!'

There wasn't much to say after that, and they eventually drifted back to the Red Lion where they said 'Thanks' and 'Goodnight' to Tony and Loada. Slim prised Graham out of an otherwise endless discussion of Crib league rules, reminding him of Eileen's strict curfew time during the working week. Boots nipped off to the Manor House in case there was a chance of a final stroll with Anna, and Whacker hung around the bar hoping for the same with Tina – but both girls had had a full, tiring day and offered no more than a gentle 'goodnight'.

Friday morning found the lads catching the 9.15 bus and being given a right royal send-off by their mothers and the ladies of their recent Charlford lives – Anna, Tina and Eileen – the latter giving the driver, husband Graham, strict instructions to drive carefully, as if he ever did otherwise.

Chapter 23

It was some three months later when a 7-seat minibus – or was it a taxi? – pulled up at the front of the Red Lion in Charlford, and Ted Bailey led the passengers out, straight into the inn for the very welcome drinks that had been arranged for their arrival. It hadn't been a bad journey from Bracknell, though they had all been ready for the comfort break at the service station outside Oxford. The driver went off to refuel the vehicle, and to get a garage to look at the heater system that had been playing up a bit, promising to be back for their planned mid-afternoon departure time.

Inside the Red Lion, the visitors warmed themselves in front of the log fire and exchanged greetings with the one or two locals they'd met before.

To the forefront of these were Graham and Eileen, both of them having arranged to be off duty that day, wanting to see how Slim and his mum were – and had Slim played any more Crib?? 'Not much,' he replied, 'only a couple of games at school, but it's been a real help with the Saturday job I got last month. I help out in a charity shop, and the mental arithmetic is great for sorting out change for people – and the older customers think it's great that I can do it – so, thanks.'

Tina was there, ostensibly to help her dad serve the refreshments, and exchanged an almost shy greeting with Whacker.

'Are you still moving here, then?' she asked. 'Is that what you've come to do?'

'Yes and no,' he replied with a smile and a blush. 'As far as I know we're definitely coming here, but today's trip is to take a final look to make sure my mum's happy with whatever has been done to the cottage, and for Dad to see the deal Mr Philips is offering. I don't get a say in it, as far as I can tell, but I'll be happy to see you more often – if that's OK with you?' And again, he blushed and looked round to see who might have heard, but everyone else was more interested in their own conversations – but he was a bit put out by her next comment. 'I can't see your friend Boots – isn't he with you?'

'Oh, he's here all right, but why the interest?'

'It's not for me, silly! It's Anna who really wanted to know if he was coming when I told her about the trip, and your dad booking refreshments and lunch for so many, but without giving names. So, where is he then – not gone straight to the Manor House has he?'

'Wouldn't be surprised, though how often they can see each other, I've no idea, but I think they've met up in Oxford once or twice.'

Elsewhere, Sarah was again thanking Eileen for looking after Slim; Ted was confirming lunch arrangements with Jim; then Detective Cole came in and turned their conversation to the possibilities of forming a Cribbage club, and of getting the carriage into use at Charlford Manor.

Seeing that Boots' mum, Pauline, was looking a bit left out, Tina approached her.

'Hello, it's Mrs Clark, isn't it? I'm Tina and it was me that almost turned the lads away when they arrived for the weekend that Mrs Bennett booked for them in August!'

'Yes, that's right,' she replied with a laugh, 'they told me about it, and I was really surprised to hear about the deception – fancy saying they were getting ready for a tour!! I know that Slim got into a bit of trouble during their stay, but I'm glad the lads didn't actually cause any – they didn't, did they?'

'No, they were fine and they brought a bit of interest to the village – there was your son winning the Tell-a-Tale contest here, as well as Slim's efforts trying to help the police. I didn't get to hear any of their music, but Anna said they were quite good.'

'Yes, I think they are, too, but I can't see the group lasting now that the Bailey family are moving here – I don't think they're good enough or established enough to justify all the travel entailed in keeping in touch. A pity, but that's life.'

She looked quite sad about it, prompting Tina to try to change the subject – 'As you know the lads so well, do you know why they all use nicknames? No Michael, Steve, Pete, or any other ordinary names?'

'No idea about the other two, but Boots was what he always said when we went near a branch of Clarks – our surname, of course – from the times we went there to get new working boots for my late husband. And I'm told that that sort of thing's not unusual – a bit like Shush Taylor the footballer – I think somebody said that happened because he was a noisy lad; his dad was a shift worker and often in bed during the day, so the lad got used to hearing "Shush, don't do that" and so he thought his name was Shush, and that's all he answered to!'

Anna had confided to Tina that she had no idea what, if anything, Boots' mum knew about her, and just didn't know how to play it if she met her, so Tina decided to tackle it head-on for her friend. 'I hope you don't mind me asking,' started Tina, 'but is this just a run out for you, or is there something in the village of particular interest? I know that some of our visitors, for instance, are here to look at aspects of the Church.'

'Well, actually I think there's a tapestry or two in the Manor House that might be worth looking at, according to Boots. I didn't notice them when I was here in August, but I think I'll ask Anna to let me see them – she and Boots are very fond of each other, you know, so I hope she won't think it's an excuse to get to know her better.'

Parents! thought Tina. How come we always underestimate them!!

This conversation was getting complicated and Tina was pleased to break it off when they saw that Ted was starting to get the group on the move down to the Manor House, so they joined in and off they all went.

The sight that greeted them as they approached the Manor was quite different from the one they mainly remembered from their visit in August. The house itself was unchanged, but the stable yard and outbuildings were largely hidden behind a collection of huts and piles of building materials, all surrounded by a tall security fence.

'We're definitely not moving here any time soon then, Dad,' remarked Whacker. 'I thought Tony was just having an extra loo put in the cottage. This looks more like a rebuild of something.'

'Don't worry, lad. I've spoken to him and seen some of the plans, and he's doing a proper job of it – no half measures.'

'But it doesn't look like the country retreat you had in mind, does it? You tell him, Mum.'

'Oh, I agree with your dad – it's all going to be OK. I know what's planned, but we didn't want to bother you with it while you're studying. Anyway, Tony's going to walk us round it all and you'll see it's going to be fine.'

The rest of the group had been included in this brief explanation and were all pleased to see Tony coming out to meet them, as promised.

'Right, folks, and welcome to the start of the new-look home of Charlford Enterprises.' Seeing the puzzled expressions on all but Ted and Alison's faces, Tony quickly continued, 'Sorry – quick explanation. Anna's birthday weekend made me realise I couldn't just sit here and enjoy the view, and Ted's interest in coming to live and work here got me thinking seriously about what I could actually do here. The upshot is that I've teamed up again with Reg Harris – the chap I was in business with before – and we've formed a sort of umbrella organisation – Charlford Enterprises. The aim is to help out with admin, advertising, recruitment and such like for smaller businesses, like Ted's. We've obviously talked it through with Ted, and with a couple of people interested in setting up in the stable buildings. We've been able to put a bit more money into renovating and upgrading the buildings here, and that's why it's taking a bit longer than we first thought.'

Cutting through the ensuing murmurings of interest and understanding, Tony continued, 'As it's still a bit of a building site, I only want to take Ted and Alison to look in detail at their potential premises, so if the rest of you don't mind going into the main house, Anna will look after you.'

Putting paternal arms around both Ted and Alison, Tony guided them towards the stable yard, carefully avoiding the odd heap of rubble, wheelbarrow and open ditch.

'You can see why I didn't want a crowd down here, eh? I persuaded the builders to have a very long morning break – I didn't want to announce your visit otherwise they'd have spent yesterday getting the place tidy instead of getting on with the job – we've already had too many hold-ups waiting for materials or for building reg approvals plus, of course, bad weather days.'

'There's certainly more stuff being done than I'd expected,' said Ted. 'What's it all for?'

'Well, the visible stuff like the trenches, they came about because, the more we looked at the idea of leasing places to businesses, the more we identified the things we'd have to provide – like mains services and toilets – the toilets have been added to the end of the stable block. Then there are those panels over there' – pointing towards the coach house – 'they're soundproofing to go on internal walls so that quiet trades – as well as the cottage and the main house – aren't affected by machine noise, loud hammering and so on. Oh, and I'd forgotten that the place has absolutely no garages – the previous owner had used the coach house that you want for a workshop, Ted, and I'd simply left my car outside round the back of the house. So, the hole in the wall at the end of the stable block, that leads to where the new garages will be – one for every work unit plus me – as well as to the toilets for use by trades and their visitors.'

Alison was first to formulate a response to all this information. 'That must have taken an awful lot of planning, as well as getting necessary approvals. I think you've done really well to achieve so much in the time.'

'That's very kind of you, Alison, but I must admit that we sailed a bit close to the wind on occasion, rather assuming we'd get an approval here and there. And it also helped having so many contacts in relevant businesses and trades –

we got quite a few odd days of effort when other jobs had hold-ups – benefits all round.'

'You've not mentioned a completion date for our needs, Tony – likely to be before Christmas, do you think? Not that I'm pushing – don't really fancy a move in bad weather – but I could use a few weeks' notice.'

'Let's show you what's been done in the cottage – I wanted that to be ready at least as soon as the work unit so you can have a base here while you move down, and I think it's not far off. Main things still to do are confirm cooking facilities and then just the decorations.'

Alison was pleased at the idea of having so little to make decisions on, but equally hoped she'd be happy with what she was about to be faced with. She needn't have worried, Tony had made sure that all the renovations were what they'd agreed, but then had a surprise on offer in the kitchen.

'It all looks fine, Tony, but where does that door lead to? I seem to remember there was a big cupboard there – I certainly couldn't manage without that amount of storage space.'

'Ah, I hope you'll agree this was a good move. We've enclosed the space between the cottage and the old laundry room to make you a scullery or a utility room – call it what you like – and this is the door to it!' and he opened it with a dramatic flourish. 'There, what do you think to that?'

'That is terrific, and you'd never know it hadn't been there all the time – thank you very much!'

But, turning back to look again into the kitchen, Alison wondered if she'd been too enthusiastic, and wondered how her next comment would be received – 'Didn't you say you'd get rid of the solid-fuel cooking range? Even Anna said it made the kitchen too hot to use in summer.'

'I know, and I agree, but it's been converted to run on either gas or solid fuel.'

'But there's no gas in the village, is there?'

'No, but there's bottled gas for the main house and I've had it extended to here – it comes over in the trench out there. If we find we use more between us than the current cylinder can cope with, the gas people tell me it'll be fairly easy to swap to a bigger one. They also recommended we do it this way rather than have an extra storage tank just for the cottage. Anyway, what do you think of it?'

'Seems good to me,' joined in Ted, 'if Alison is happy – OK, love? But what's it cost and how do we pay for it?'

'Well, it's all at standard rates suggested by the gas people and you get your own meter so you can monitor it – then you pay me, along with the rent. If you use solid fuel in winter, then you get it wherever you want – if I can get a bulk price for the big house, you can get that from me too, but that's up to you. Like it's up to you if you use the range or bring in any separate cookers. OK?'

'Well, that seems fine, Tony, but can I try the range using gas while we're here – just turn on a burner to see what it feels like?'

'Of course you can – it's all set up and has automatic ignition, so you'll only need matches when you use solid fuel. The instruction manual's in that drawer, so have a study and see what you make of it.'

Ted and Tony moved to the kitchen window and realised that the builders were trickling back to work, earlier than Tony had expected. 'Best get a move on,' he said, 'before we find ourselves up to our necks in dust and muck and very much in the way.'

Alison had found the right page in the booklet, but the stove didn't want to light, so first Tony then Ted had a go.

'Perhaps it got turned off at the meter,' said Tony. 'If we all go and turn it on, you can have a look at the set-up in there, then we can come back and light the stove properly, then get out of the way of the builders.'

Acknowledging the greetings of one or two chaps on the way, Tony led them to what had been a small coal shed, attached to the one-time laundry room.

'It seemed appropriate to put the power meters in here as it used to be the coal house – the coal was dropped in through that hatch, but I'm having a window put in there. In the old days, I guess they didn't need a light or they'd bring a lantern when they were shovelling coal into scuttles and buckets. The previous owner put a simple light in, and had the sense to use a pull cord switch – easy to find in the dark and it didn't matter if it got dirty, but it could be a bit temperamental. Anyway, it's all been rewired to modern standards.'

'What else will the place be used for?' asked Ted. 'Can anybody come in and mess about with our supplies?'

'Oh, no, Ted. There'll only be three keys – one each for you and whoever has use of the laundry room, plus a master kept in the house. It'll be as secure as a meter cupboard on the side of a house and not as noticeable. No-one's taken an interest in the laundry room yet, but I'll make sure any tenants are responsible, don't you fret. And as for other uses, I reckon you could keep yard brooms and such like – up to you, really.'

'Let's have a look at this meter, then,' said Alison, keen to check out the cooker.

Tony unlocked the door and reached inside for the new light switch – click – nothing happened. Feeling around the switch, he realised it had no cables going to it.

'Looks like they fitted the switch ready for the cables, but didn't get that far. Never mind, let's see if they left the original pull switch connected,' and he waved his arm around where he remembered it had been. 'Well, at least the cord's still here, so let's hope it works or I'll have to go up to the house for a torch.'

At the first pull nothing happened, so Tony pulled the cord again, a little bit harder and this produced a small crackling sound in the body of the switch as a loose earth wire touched a live one.

But Tony didn't hear that as it was drowned by the flash and bang as the small pocket of escaped gas exploded.

Nor did he feel the massive push of the explosion, but he certainly experienced it as he was flung backwards out of the coal house door to land on his back in the yard outside.

From that small spark onwards, Tony's world was black and silent.

Chapter 24

Again, after a gap of a further three months, a 7-seat minibus – or was it a taxi? – arrived in Charlford and pulled up, not at the Red Lion, but at the front door of the Manor House, and again it was Ted Bailey who led the passengers out. Again, it hadn't been a bad journey from Bracknell, and again they had all been ready for the comfort break at the service station outside Oxford. And, as before, the driver went off to refuel the vehicle ready for the afternoon's return journey.

Before Ted reached the front door, it was opened, and there was Tony Philips – not quite as they remembered him, but certainly in better condition than some of them had feared after the accident last November. He was smiling and looked healthy, but he was in a wheelchair and had a brace thing around his neck – he could have looked worse but, of course, they'd have preferred him to look a whole lot better.

'Welcome, Team Bracknell! Welcome back to the home of Charlford Enterprise,' he called, with a broad smile that helped ease any concerns that their visit might not be as welcome as Ted had led them to believe. 'Come on in and get some warm refreshment inside you!'

Without any pre-planning, the ladies went in first, each exchanging a warm handshake with Tony; then came the lads with high fives, and finally Ted with a long-held double handshake.

The appearance and state of the interior of the Manor House had changed and improved a lot since their previous visit, thanks mainly to the efforts of Tony's friend and partner Reg Harris and his wife Lynda.

Reg had been at the house at the time of the explosion, waiting to be introduced to Ted when Tony would explain the creation of Charlford Enterprises. So, once the emergency services gave permission for things to be moved and so on, he'd taken charge. On a personal level, he'd got Lynda to go to the hospital and look after Anna as she waited for Tony's injuries to be assessed and treated – Lynda had then brought Anna home and moved in to help her and Mrs W to run the house etc.

On a business level, when the owners of the gas and electrical contractors at the heart of the incident said they wanted to do something to make amends, he got them to carry out, or pay for, items that would make the place easier to run and homelier for when Tony would be back convalescing. This, of course, had to be without compromising any insurance claims or legal obligations that would be clarified when the health and safety people carried out their detailed investigation. This investigation eventually established that the light switch that caused the escaped gas to explode was in the process of being replaced when the electrician was called away to another job – unfortunately he'd already marked the job sheet to say he'd done it, so no-one had checked.

'I can't tell you how pleased I am to be back and seeing you up and about again, Tony,' said Ted. 'I know you've said you're fine over the phone, but you gave us a real fright last time. Are you sure you're up to it – showing us all over the place and signing me up?'

'Don't worry, Ted, it's not as bad as it looks. I don't really need the chair – well, not all the time – but Anna fusses over me and I don't want to worry her any more than necessary. She's been absolutely wonderful – and so have the Wilkinsons. Don't know what I'd have done without them.'

'You mean both Wilkinsons are here?' asked Ted, his eyebrows shooting up in genuine surprise. 'Surely Mr W was in line for some court appearances and probably serious penalties. Things must really have changed an awful lot for you to trust him back inside the Manor House!'

'Long story, Ted, and I think it would be best for you to hear it from them – I'm sure to get something wrong! Ah, speak of the devil, here's Mrs W armed with refreshments for the weary travellers, so don't keep her too long.' With that, he wheeled himself off to the drawing room where the rest of the visitors were wandering round.

'Yes, sir, what can I help you with?' asked Mrs W, startling Ted who'd not been addressed as 'sir' for some time.

'Well, I feel a bit embarrassed about this,' he replied. 'You see, to be honest, I was surprised that your husband was here in the household, considering the cloud he was under when we were here last summer and Mr Philips suggested I'd best ask you about it – but it's er, more than cheeky, I suppose to ask you outright like he suggests, so let's forget it and just be pleased that things have worked out for you. And let's not keep you stood there holding that try.'

'Oh, we don't mind telling people about it if they ask – it just clears the air. Let me take the tray in, sir, and I'll tell you all about our little episode whenever it's convenient to you. Is that all right?'

'Yes, of course – but please don't keep calling me sir. If all goes to plan and we move here, you and I will be on the same footing, more or less – both depending on Mr Philips for our livelihoods.'

'Very good, Mr Bailey,' she replied, with a smile that settled the matter.

Following Mrs W into the drawing room, Ted saw that Anna was already there, chatting happily with Boots and his mum. Slim and Whacker were in deep conversation looking out of one of the windows towards the stable yard, and their mothers were studying the furnishings and pictures that had been added to the room since their last visit.

Playing the proper young hostess, Anna came straight over to Ted to welcome him again to Charlford Manor.

'Hello, Anna, or should I address you as Miss Anna, as I believe the Wilkinsons do?' he asked with a smile.

'Whatever are you talking about, Mr Bailey?' she asked. 'OK, Mr and Mrs W do call me Miss Anna, even though I try to get them not to; but why ever should you do the same?'

'Oh, it's just a bit of nonsense I was sharing with Mrs W, who kept calling me "sir" – you know how she is. Anyway, I tried to put it to her that she and I were on the same footing – both relying on your dad for our livelihoods – and I think she sort of accepted that, so I'm now Mr Bailey – sometimes to be followed by a "sir", if I know the lady!'

They both laughed, then Ted continued, 'It's great to see your father looking well, despite the wheelchair, and this room looking so nice. Before we came in, it smelled like something really tasty was on the go in the kitchen, so shouldn't you or Mrs W be keeping an eye on it, instead of taking care of us intruders?'

'That's Kelly – if Dad didn't tell you about her, I'll get him to deal with it now while I circulate a bit more.' With that, and leaving Ted puzzled, Anna went and had a quiet word with Tony who excused himself from Slim and his mum to join Ted.

This was the part of the day that Tony was seriously not looking forward to. He'd been approached a few weeks before by Kelly, asking if she could rent the old laundry room for her sandwich and hot snack business, Kelly's Kitchen. She explained that it had started off just as a sandwich delivery service for small businesses – mainly offices and trading estates – that didn't have easy access to shops and cafes and such. But it soon became successful and customers were now asking for soups, sausage rolls and other items that needed cooking, and she'd fully outgrown her – though actually her mother's – kitchen.

While Tony was pleased at the prospect of yet another paying tenant, he knew that not all cooking smells would be acceptable to people – himself included. So, after some thought, he agreed a temporary tenancy but with restrictions on timings – no cooking after 11am – and on ingredients – no garlic and no curries – and this would have to be acceptable to other tenants. This suited Kelly, but would it suit Ted and, more importantly, his wife Alison? He was about to find out.

'Well, Ted, I'm afraid this is where I put you – and you, Alison – on the spot a bit. You see, I've got a new tenant – on a temporary basis – in the old laundry room.' And he went on to explain the situation, ending with, 'So if you're not happy about any of this, just say so and I'll sort it out. And don't worry, Kelly fully understands the situation.'

The Baileys looked at each other in puzzlement for a full half a minute before Ted, looking between Alison and Tony, at last spoke. 'I don't see the problem, Tony. It's just cooking smells like any house would have from time to time, you've put a reasonable time limit on it and, after all, it's your property to rent out as you wish. What do you say, Alison?'

'Oh, I agree with you, Ted. And she might easily find a couple of new customers on her doorstep when I go off out for the day leaving you and Whacker to fend for yourselves. Sounds like a good thing, to me.'

'But what about the other crafts people?' asked Ted. 'Didn't you say on the phone that you'd got a saddler and – was it a weaver? – down in the old stable block; what do they say?'

'Oh, they're happy enough – and they're now Kelly's customers too – but they don't get the veto.'

'Sorry, Tony – what's this about a veto? We wouldn't want to put the mockers on somebody's business just because we might not always like their cooking smells. Why would our tastes be so important? – But wait a minute, are we all to be part of Charlford Enterprises and have a say in each other's activities like some sort of co-operative, 'cause if we are, I'm not sure I'm happy about it.'

Alison looked between the two men and felt a little sick. She knew how much Ted wanted this move to this location to be successful – he'd never really been a town sort of chap – and they'd put so much thought and effort into making the decision and then planning for the move.

Tony had perhaps seen this response coming, and jumped in quickly.

'No, Ted, it's no co-operative, and we've actually changed the name from "Enterprises" to just "Enterprise". It's just me and Reg's enterprise, you know, to provide premises or services to small businesses like you. But you've got the main say on what happens in the yard because you're the main tenant there and your home's there, so that's the main thing that's affected. Hope that's cleared it up?'

To Alison's relief, Ted nodded to show his acceptance. 'But you're not going to keep roping me in on other decisions, are you? Keeping away from that sort of stuff is why I like working for myself.'

'No, it won't be like that, only if something might have an impact on your home. For instance, when Reg was getting some furnishings and decorations – and, of course, the chairlift – to bring in here, mainly from house clearances, he got the idea he'd like to see about setting up an auction house! Now that would be part of the group, but not affect you here at all.'

'Unless it brought me some cabinets to work on,' laughed Ted.

'Funny you should mention that, Ted. Remember the parcels of books we found in the carriage?' Nods all round. 'Well, Reg came across them and felt they'd be good for an auction, but I reckon I'd rather have them looking good in bookshelves in the sitting room. So we may be after you to build something in due course – you up for it?'

Ted's happy smile was all the answer Tony needed, and did a power of good for Alison's confidence that they were doing the right thing in moving.

'Well, there you are then, Ted, we'll all look out for each other without being a co-operative – how does that suit?'

'That seems fine, so let's just get on and sign things – OK, Alison?'

His wife readily agreed, feeling even more happy about the move, but she had her own queries for Tony.

'You and Anna will still be living here, in the Manor House, won't you, Tony? I've sometimes imagined it could be a bit isolated and perhaps lonely down here in the cottage.'

'Oh yes, we plan to be here, and Anna is no longer boarding at school. And, for the moment, the Wilkinsons are in residence too, but none of us are sure how long that will last.'

'It seems to me, then,' said Alison, 'that if the cottage is as we expect it to be, and if you two agree on the terms for it and the workshop, we could sign and settle it all today. What do you think, Ted?'

'Just what I was thinking, so can we get out and have a look at things, Tony?'

'Ready when you are, but let's get people organised a bit so we stay connected.'

So as to be heard above the quiet murmur of various conversations, Tony raised his voice a little to announce, 'If you can finish off your refreshments, I've arranged for us all to see into all the work areas, including those in use, then for the Bailey family to have a proper look at the cottage. After that, if we can be back in here by about 12.30, there'll be a light lunch of soup and a roll provided by Kelly – that's probably the soup you can smell at the moment – followed by a sandwich and a piece of cake produced by my clever daughter, Anna.' Here he was interrupted by her plaintive cry of, 'Oh, Dad, please don't!' But he continued amid a ripple of laughter, 'Ably, and perhaps necessarily!! supervised by Mrs W.'

This was greeted with a ripple of applause, followed by chatter as they all looked to form groups for the tour. After a minute or two, Tony got their attention again and suggested they all go around first as a single group before splitting up to revisit any parts of particular interest. Thus it was that, about five minutes later, they were all outside and Tony led them into the stable yard.

'We won't go into the cookhouse while Kelly's working, but if anyone needs to see in there, I'm sure she'll show you round after lunch.'

Tony then guided them to the coach houses, the first of them sitting ready for Ted's tools and materials to arrive, the others looking clean and tidy and suitable for a whole range of businesses.

'Excuse me, Tony,' interrupted Whacker, 'but I can't help noticing there's no carriage around here – what happened to it, please?'

'Oh, yes, should have mentioned it. You'll be happy to know it's in good hands, ready to be refurbished for use next year. Detective Cole and his mates think have found a stable with a couple of horses all trained up to pull coaches, and they can store it for them so it won't be coming back here. Anyway, they plan to use it for pleasure and perhaps even display it at country shows and the like. From what they tell me, it should be something special.'

'Great, eh Dad? Look forward to seeing that.'

Turning to go towards the stable block, Whacker stopped in his tracks and asked, 'What happened here, Tony? You've not rebuilt the stables, have you? They don't look the same as when I was in there working on the drum kit.'

'Oh no, lad, this was an easy transformation, but it's made a heck of a difference inside. All we had to do was build the wall along the front between the supporting pillars, and put doors and windows in, of course. The corridor it created, means they can have the studio doors open to get more light in without letting the heat out.'

Going into the stable block, they looked in on the saddler and then the lady working in wool. Each had its own aroma and atmosphere that carried a warmth despite the chill of the day. Both of the workers were happy to see occasional visitors and invited anyone interested to call back to see more or have a chat.

Moving along the corridor that linked the stables, Tony showed the visitors the washrooms that had been created from an old feed store and tack room.

'These are for the traders and their visitors, so you won't have people knocking on the cottage door asking for the loo, Alison!'

'Thank goodness for that,' she laughed, 'though it's something I'd never thought about.'

Taking them out through a separate door, Tony spread his arms to indicate an expanse of vegetable garden, and said, 'Now here's something that I'd never thought about. This was the Manor House kitchen garden, but I'd not really looked at it, let alone given any thought to its use. Then Kelly saw it one day and asked if her brother could rent it to grow veg, some for her and some for sale – under the heading, Kelly's Crops. Doubtless that will be advertised as Crops with a K! I got the builders to put that gateway through the wall for easy access and the garden's being brought back to life – or at least it's starting to. There's still a fair bit of clearing up to do and we started a bit late for him to grow much from seed for this year, but he brought some seedlings along and I reckon it's going to be productive for them.'

'Looks like I'll be signing up as a regular customer here as well as at Kelly's Kitchen,' said Alison, 'so we won't miss having much of a garden of our own, Ted.' A sentiment with which he agreed whole-heartedly.

'Right, folks,' said Tony, 'this is where the guided bit of the tour ends, so have a look around at whatever you like while I take the Bailey's to look at the cottage – see you all back in the house about 12.30, OK?'

'Before you go, Tony,' interrupted Whacker, 'we've not seen any garages.'

'Oh, yes, young man, worried about where to store your drums, I imagine,' and laughed. 'Well, I had to change plans when I realised we could bring the kitchen garden back into use – that's where I thought they'd go. Now the architect and surveyor are looking at different locations. But it will get sorted and, for the moment, the bits of the drum kit you left here are all on the mezzanine floor in your dad's workshop. OK? Now we really must get moving.'

So saying, he led Alison and Tony back and into the cottage where Alison made straight for the cooking range. 'You're sure it's OK to try it this time, Tony?' she asked, fairly seriously – the memory of the explosion at their last visit was still strong in her mind.

'Let me do it, love,' interrupted Ted, fully understanding her concern. 'I need to know how to work it anyway for those days when you're off gallivanting in Salchester!' And the slight tension was dispelled by their smiles.

Of course, the cooker worked properly, as did the lights, and the heating system. And they checked that the bathroom and other plumbed areas were all finished to the high standards that Tony had promised.

'What do you think, then, love?' Ted asked Alison. 'OK to sign up and get on with the move?'

'Oh, I'm happy with the cottage if you are, but what about the workshop?'

'More than happy there, and it looks as if it'll be clear for Whacker to transfer over to Salchester College after the Christmas break. So, Tony, we're ready to sign if you are.'

'Sure thing.' A firm handshake sealed the deal, then, 'Look at the time! Let's get back to the house for some lunch, then we can get the paperwork signed, OK?'

Back in the Manor House the rest of the group were being ushered by the Wilkinsons to seats at the tables set up in the dining room, the main places having been reserved for Tony, Anna, Alison and Ted. Whacker was already seated at another table with Slim and Boots, and when he spotted where his parents were sitting, he couldn't help calling out, in a mock hurt tone, 'All right, Dad, I know my place – unpaid, unloved, uninvited to the party!' This got the laugh he expected, and the room then settled down to the serious business of enjoying a lunch they'd not really expected.

As they were all polishing off the last of the cake – and they all agreed Anna had made a good job of it – Mr W came in to tell Tony that the other guests had arrived and been shown in to the drawing room. This announcement was obviously a surprise to Ted and Alison so, before they could ask about it, Tony got everyone's attention.

'I'm sure you won't mind, but I've invited in several of the friends you've made on previous visits – they wanted to see you again and there wouldn't be time today for you to go around the village to meet them all. And while they're here they can also see a bit of what's happening.'

The first ones going into the drawing room were Slim and his mum, Sarah, looking to catch up on news with Graham and Eileen; but their first question was about Mr W – what had happened at his trial and how come he was here in the Manor House as large as life?

Fortunately, DC Cole was near enough to hear this, so was able to give the complete answer. 'When the silly man was caught he was just trying to get to the bottom of the mystery of the jewellery before he brought it to the police. He'd had his suspicions – and it turns out he was right – that somebody in the family had pulled a flanker and defrauded an insurance company when they claimed the jewellery had been stolen – and they'd inflated its value as well. It seems there'd been a genuine set – quite valuable – and a set of copied pieces that were used on a more or less day-to-day basis. I can't disclose how the scam was worked, but Mr W wasn't trying to sell the stuff that day, he just wanted to check its value so he'd know which set it was, and whether it confirmed his suspicions or not. That was all proved and accepted and he got off with a very mild caution – helped a lot by character statements from some very influential people the pair had worked for over the years.'

'So that bit of menacing stuff he acted out to me was just that, then – acting?' asked Slim.

'Yes, it really was, but it probably came out more authentic on account of the state of his nerves – he was trembling like a leaf when we got to him!'

Mrs Wilkinson had soon forgiven her husband for the scare he'd given her, but she'd wanted to show Tony Philips her appreciation for how he had come to her aid when Mr W was arrested. Tony was really grateful to have her helping him run the house and to give Anna any housekeeping tips and advice she needed. To avoid any problems, Mrs W persuaded her husband to stay away, so he went off to visit a couple of the places that were on their original plans, and waited for when his wife was ready for them to team up again and move off.

'So that's why she was here at the time of the explosion, then?' asked Slim, still somewhat aggrieved at how he felt Mr W had put the wind up him when he retrieved the jewels, and how embarrassed he, Slim, had felt in reporting that to the police.

'Yes,' continued Loada, 'and, according to Tony, after the explosion and what he calls his "little tumble", she was happy to become a semi-permanent member of domestic staff. And he says he was more than happy to have Mr W join her when he was totally cleared of all charges soon after the accident.'

'And as I often say,' interrupted Tony, who'd overheard the end of that conversation, 'I don't know what I'd have done without them. By the way, Detective, have you told Master Bennett the latest on his attacker?'

Seeing Slim's look of alarm, Loada quickly said, 'Not to worry – is it still Slim? Right, well you'll not see any more of that thug Jerry Doyle. We reckon you were right not to press charges – it gave us the chance to keep an eye on him, and it paid off. We were able to identify the gang that were using him for info, collared them on their next job, and they're about to be put away for a while. The judge reckoned that Doyle really was being used and deserved another chance, and we supported that, particularly as the family was about to move a long way away from our patch. So you'll not see him again, but thanks for what you did in helping us find him.'

Both Slim and his mum, Sarah, were relieved and very happy to hear all that, as Slim had hoped he'd be coming to the area visiting the friends he'd made here.

Boots' mum, Pauline, had come over with Boots and Anna, and interrupted to ask about the chairlift running up the side of the stairs. 'I can understand that being very useful as long as you need the wheelchair, Tony, but what will you do with it when you're walking unaided again?'

'I know it's quite an investment,' interrupted Sarah. 'We often arrange for them for ex-servicemen and their families – oops, sorry, none of my business, only I've come across quite a few cases where they couldn't get much back, if anything, when it was no longer needed.'

'Oh, don't worry about the cost – we were very lucky to get it second hand – or "pre-loved" as the glossy magazines put it these days! As you say, not many people take them on, mainly because there's no guarantee of their condition and how well they've been maintained. But we were lucky here that one of the chaps that had worked on this one had just joined Reg's workshop team. He could confirm it was in good nick when Reg was approached to take it away as part of a house clearance.'

'That was a stroke of luck,' continued Sarah. 'So I suppose it doesn't really matter how long you keep it, as long as it doesn't do any lasting damage to the staircase wall.'

'It's not going anywhere just yet, Sarah,' Tony replied, 'it's already booked for use in a couple of weeks' time! I don't know if they told you, but the Wilkinsons are another aspect of Charlford Enterprise, and they are going to need it!'

And he paused and smiled at the expected looks of shock, surprise and puzzlement all around. By this time, all the Bracknell group had joined the locals, had exchanged greetings, and everyone was wondering what the next item on the agenda would be. But having got their attention, Tony just hoped he was up to making a proper job of what he wanted to achieve, but he took a deep breath and plunged in.

What Tony hadn't explained, and didn't plan to, was that this invitation wasn't entirely for the benefit of the Bracknell contingent. Immediately after the explosion there had been a lot of interest in the Manor House and his plans, all stemming from the press coverage of the incident. This included a statement from the county fire and rescue service that it was entirely an accident caused by a spark in a faulty light switch igniting a small pocket of gas that had escaped from a tiny leak in a gas pipe. They naturally took the opportunity to remind people to have all their gas appliances checked regularly by qualified engineers – the fact that this message got home to people was shown by the sudden increase in demand for such checks. They had also told Tony that most of the force of the blast had escaped through the open door, and it was just his misfortune to have been stood in the way of it.

Whilst this newspaper coverage acted as free publicity for the business plan, it gave rise to the idea that a visitor attraction was being developed. Although statements to the local papers denied this, many of those involved in the work at the Manor House reported back that people still thought that at least a craft centre with café, etc., would soon be opened. So, the visit of Ted and friends was seen as an opportunity to get some local villagers in to see and hear what was happening, and through them to get the word out to the community at large. Tony and Reg felt that, even if they'd tried, they couldn't have chosen to spread the word with a better group than a policeman, a publican, mobile librarian and a bus driver!!

'As you know,' he continued, 'the main thing to be done today is to confirm Ted's plan to move here and take over the cottage and set up his cabinetmaking business here – and that's what's happened, I'm very happy to say – though the crafty beggar still hasn't signed anything!!' And that got the laughter he'd hoped for and helped him relax a little.

'But I don't think Ted realises how much his interest in coming here has meant to me – and to Anna, of course. It all goes back to Anna's birthday weekend when I couldn't really answer when somebody – I think it was one of you lads – asked what I planned to do with the place. I'd actually begun to consider selling up and having another think about what to do with myself. All the stuff I needed the lads to help me with just showed how I wasn't coping. Then your interest in coming here, Ted, was like a light at the end of the tunnel and got me thinking clearly and positively again.'

'I'm glad you didn't say that at the time, Tony,' laughed a very relieved Ted, 'or we might have had second thoughts – too much pressure!'

'Anyway, I talked it over a bit with my old mate Reg, here – or at least he got me talking – when I went to the yard for those dollies to move the carriage. He came up with the idea of the sort of almost parent company that we now call Charlford Enterprise, under Reg and me.'

'Dad,' interrupted Anna, 'do we all really need to know this?'

'Well, I only want to try to clear up some stuff that the local papers have got wrong and don't seem to want to put right. But I'll try to keep it brief. First off, we want to be clear that there's not going to be any visitor attraction here – the only visitors that will be welcomed are customers of the various businesses based here, plus of course their suppliers, friends and families, and if those of you who live locally can spread that word we'd all be most grateful.'

Seeing one or two of the villagers looking a bit puzzled, even concerned, Tony quickly continued, 'And, of course, all of you invited here today are classed as friends and are welcome to visit – unless Ted or any of the other crafts people complain!!'

'So how big is Charlford Enterprise?' asked Ted. 'And what sort of benefits does it offer? And most important, what's it going to cost me?'

'To keep it brief, the only cost, on top of rent and fuels, will be if anybody uses the services we plan to offer, such as accounts, advertising, help with recruitment, and so on.'

'You should think about using some of that, Ted,' Alison was heard to whisper. 'Worth it to save you some late nights, I imagine.'

'As for how big the set-up is, at the moment it's the trades working here, plus a new engineering workshop that Reg is starting at his yard, PLUS the Wilkinsons!'

Tony waited for the gasps – and a couple of people saying 'What?' – to quieten down, then continued, 'For the past month or so, Mr and Mrs W have been helping a staff agency in Salchester by giving specialised training to some of their people. Most have been for caterers for events such as posh weddings, but one or two have been for domestic situations, and one of their next ones will include helping someone who has a stairlift!'

This was greeted with a round of applause for Mr and Mrs W who blushed and gestured a 'thank you' around the room.

'And to be absolutely clear from the start, because Ted and family will be living on site, as it were, they'll share with Reg and me the final say on what's allowed and what's not, such as noise, working hours and so on. Mind you, Ted isn't immune to this – as he's already aware, and has agreed to accept, there are strict limits on timings for operating noisy machines.'

'That means I'll get him home in time for his evening meal more often, then!' muttered Alison, to chuckles all round. 'Thanks, Tony!'

'But, as a special thanks to Ted, he's getting a discount on everything for the first few months here, so I hope that sweetens the pill of the restrictions.'

'You never mentioned this before, Tony!' replied a surprised-looking Ted. 'What's the "special thanks" for?'

'When I was first recovering after the explosion, they told me that I could have been in a worse state if you hadn't been there and made sure nobody moved me and perhaps made my back injury worse. On top of that, I started thinking back to how we got to where we are anyway, and I realised it all stemmed from you wanting to move here. So that's how I see it – where we are now, and what the future looks like – all stems from you, Ted.'

Before Ted could muster a response to this totally unexpected statement, he was surrounded by mutters of 'Hear, hear', 'Well said', 'Blow me!', and a smattering of applause.

'Hang on a bit, Tony,' said Ted, holding up his hand for a bit of hush, 'if you really want to find the trigger point, it goes back a lot further – to when the lads here, The Acolytes, were backpacking in the woods the other side of the village. I'm told it was a cold wet autumn evening, and one of them said he'd rather be staying B & B in Charlford – and that's how it all started.'

This really prompted little conversations among the guests, and Tony couldn't help but agree – 'Yes, Ted, and that led them here, and I've still not got rid of the last odds and ends of that wretched drum kit!!'

The ensuing laughter was halted when Slim raised his hand and called out, 'Sorry folks, wrong again!' earning a puzzled look from his mum.

'That incident that Mr Bailey just mentioned,' he continued, 'was more or less an exact repeat of something that happened quite a few years ago. You've all heard us talk about our heroes, the Mystic Wizards – well they used to go backpacking like we've done, but their area was around Charlbury. In fact, as it's only a few miles away, some of you older folks may have seen them. Anyway, on a similar sort of cold wet evening, one of them – and nobody's sure who it was – said he'd rather be staying B & B in Charlbury, so they did, and that's what inspired us to be here. It's also how that village became their spiritual home.'

No-one could challenge that, so it was accepted that the whole of this story was inspired by the Mystic Wizards.

The End

Acknowledgements

Top of the list are the Mystic Wizards – Ian, Kev & Paul (in alphabetical order) – whose exploits inspired me to start writing this set of books, and helping me create the outline of my fictional band. Above all, their music has provided a unique background to my family life for many years.

Son Ian created the cover illustration for the Red Lion from my imprecise description, then did amazing work editing my text, before preparing the files for the on-line publishing process.

Sincere thanks also to the staff at the Sleaford Library of Greenwich Leisure Limited, who explained the Dewey Decimal System that shows the classification of non-fiction books in a library, and supported and encouraged my writings.

About the Author

W. Henry Barnes began his writing career many years ago as a Technical Author in the UK defence electronics industry.
Since retiring to Lincolnshire, he has published two novels around the fictional village of Charlford with a third (and final one, he says) in hand.
Away from writing, he is an active member of the Lincolnshire branch of the REME Association, and keeps mind and body in trim playing bowls at a local indoor club.

Printed in Great Britain
by Amazon